KURT VONNEGUT'S
SLAUGHTERHOUSE–FIVE:
BOOKMARKED

The *Bookmarked* Series

Kurt Vonnegut's *Slaughterhouse–Five:*

BOOKMARKED

CURTIS SMITH

Kirby Gann, *Series Editor*

NEW YORK, NY

Printed in the United Sates of America.
First Paperback Edition
10 9 8 7 6 5 4 3 2 1

Please direct inquiries to:
Ig Publishing
Box 2547
New York, NY 10163
www.igpub.com

ISBN: 978-1-63246-011-0

To the uncounted, forgotten by the writers of history

So it goes. . . .

Perhaps the most often-quoted line from American literature, or at least a close second to Melville's "Call me Ishmael," Vonnegut's melancholy refrain is readily expressed by anyone reacting to bad news on a scale so large and devastating as to be abstract. No author has managed to wring so many levels of meaning and allusion, or trigger so many different feelings, from the repetitive statement of three simple words as Vonnegut has in *Slaughterhouse-Five,* arguably the novel for which he is best known. It's a musical motif that falls just short of being a chant, the echo to each instance of death and decay that appears in the novel's dark pages—over 100 times in scarcely more than 200 pages—a *memento mori* that reverberates among the numerous storylines and punctuates the author's absurdist sense of humor.

The book is a bit of a Trojan horse: its slim spine denies it the heft of those works typically anointed *classic* status, and on those few pages swims an abundance of white space, too, leaving room for scribbled illustrations no more detailed than doodles. A reader can be forgiven for thinking going in that here's a novel that can be sped through in a couple of hours for a quick fix of entertainment—maybe *provocative* entertainment, going on what people say about Vonnegut's writing—but entertainment nonetheless, and hopefully a few laughs along the way. The text encourages us to read in that way, the narrator/author opening his tale with a series of jokes and limericks and dismissive commentary on what he has prepared for us to read. And then he gets us, lightly alluding to the inescapable processes of war and inscribing in precise strokes of detail horrific images of mankind's inhumanity to itself—even as he maintains that superficially breezy tone. Our eyes slow down to make certain we don't miss anything. Billy Pilgrim has been cast out of linear time and thus we're in a jumble of past-present-future along with him, with nothing to hold on to save a tenuous faith in our charming, intermittent narrator. It's the kind of novel that can transform what a reader expects from the category, widening yet again the scope of the umbrella that covers all texts classified as The Novel. And it's fun. Moreover, if one is open to such possibilities, the story of Billy Pilgrim and the Trafalmadorians (who can sense and observe in four dimensions and see time as one simultaneous present) can change how one views the world.

It helps to be young and impressionable. For Curtis Smith the encounter came in his early teens, as he makes clear early on. As best as he can remember it, at least—he confesses to being unable to recall the day he bought the novel (the original copy of which he still owns, bound with tape and rubber bands). In this far-ranging exploration of Vonnegut's novel and its ramifications and repercussions in his own life and the wider world, Smith goes all-in Trafalmadorian himself, half imagining, half remembering his first reading of *Slaughterhouse-Five* and using it as the springboard from which to dive into many of the threads and themes presented in the novel. A history of destruction, and our intrinsic talent for cruelty; the effects, form, and nature of memory, and the love between parent and child; the moral and ethical betrayals we all endure and try to evade as we each attempt to build a life of our own, preferably without destroying the lives of others.

In a spirit similar to that of his literary subject, Curtis Smith draws on the unavoidable and blunt pain of the world in history, from the smiting of Sodom to the invasion of Iraq, as material for constructing a resonant work of contemplative art.

It makes for an excellent introduction to the Bookmarked project, a series of brief volumes in which we look to showcase authors who offer a unique consideration of a single classic literary work, preferably one that has helped shape their own writing and sensibility; not necessarily an essay readied for the academic audience—no theory required here—but an offbeat approach to literature's expansive conversation, an example of how books can form (and inform) the visions of those who write them.

Kirby Gann
Series Editor
February 2016

"There is nothing intelligent to say about a massacre."

Slaughterhouse-Five

I can only imagine.
   No, I can't.

   I found a picture. Cinder blocks propping long metal beams, the open space beneath, oxygen for the flames. Atop the beams, stacked bodies. Forty, fifty, more. Feet and hands. A child, and I look away. I wanted to draw the scene, but I can't. Sadder still—the picture isn't one of a kind. It's an echo. A turn of the wheel.

   Here's what I'll draw—a frame. Fill it how you like. How you must. God bless us all.

*

"All this happened, more or less."

The first line of *Slaughterhouse-Five* is a trickster's greeting, a fitting introduction from a guide as charming as he is sly. With these words, Kurt Vonnegut opens a door, and as we cross the threshold, we enter a realm dimly lit and full of mirrors, a set built with the warped architecture of dreams. The door shuts. We've entered the slaughterhouse, and the only exit leads to a moonscape of smoking rubble.

In the first chapter, Vonnegut (or the character who claims to be Vonnegut) travels back to Dresden, the city whose destruction he witnessed as a POW. He brings a book with him—Erika Ostrovsky's *Céline and His Vision*. Céline was a soldier wounded in World War I, and upon his return home, he suffered sleeplessness and auditory hallucinations. At night, while those untouched by the war dreamt, he penned grotesque novels. He wrote, "No art is possible without a dance with death."

There is death in *Slaughterhouse-Five*, death on almost every page. Some are deaths of individuals, others occur in the thousands. So it goes. The dance goes round and round, picking up partners along the way. The dance swirls through time and space. Our partner is a master, light on his feet, as old as time itself, and when he whispers in our ear, we smile at the absurdity of all that has come before. Death holds us close, and when we return the embrace, we understand the hollowness of worldly desires and the foolishness of men, their stupidity, their brutality. We laugh. What else can we do?

*

The focus of *Slaughterhouse-Five* is the firebombing of Dresden. Vonnegut claims 135,000 men, women, and children were incinerated; other estimates place the tally closer to 30,000. Exact numbers are impossible—the city, thought safe by many, was full of refugees. A population uncounted. The destruction so complete.

Some contend the first, and most complete, massacre inflicted upon humankind occurred around 2350 BC with the Great Flood. Listen to Genesis 7: 21-22: "And all flesh died that moved upon the earth, both fowl, and of cattle, and of beast, and of every creeping thing that creepeth upon the earth, and every man: all in whose nostrils was the breath of life, of all that was in the dry land, died."

Drowning often makes lists of the most-feared ways to die. A drowning man will attempt to hold his breath until he gives over to the breathing reflex. Consciousness can linger for minutes. The panic is thought to be terrifying.

I can imagine all those people beneath the water thinking, *Please help me, God!*

*

The Ardmore Bookstore was nestled in a long brick row, the same block as the Army-Navy and a generations-old theater destined to fade in the coming age of multiplexes. I lived a little over a mile away, a walk through blue-collar neighborhoods just outside Philly's city line. Our neighborhood white, the bordering neighborhood black, a passing made with caution. Sometimes words were exchanged, sometimes I ran. The cruelty of children.

Forty years have passed. I see my sneakers on baking July sidewalks. I see them kicking brown leaves and sliding over powdery snow. All trips become one trip, a trick of memory. I am thirteen, fourteen, fifteen. There's money in my pocket—singles and quarters. Perhaps a five. I am alone or with a friend or two. Those different times, my house left with only the promise to be back by dinner.

A parking lot sat behind the bookstore. The terrain on a gentle slant, the spaces filled on weekend nights for the theater's latest films. A hundred parking meters, a hundred sundial shadows, thin stains that stretched longer as the afternoon wore on. Of course the bookstore had a front entrance, the wide sidewalk, the avenue's bustle, but I preferred the back. A simple sign, a clandestine portal. A bell on the door. The hallway a cramped passage. A choking of boxes, deliveries and returns. The store long and narrow, the shelves running parallel from front to back. The space brighter in the front. The counter with the register, its newspapers for sale. The plate glass window that looked upon Lancaster Avenue. Behind the register, the owners, the husband or wife or sometimes both, a quiet couple, their attention often on the books they read between ringing up customers.

No scent of brewing coffee flavored the air, no music played. Only stillness and the hushed voices of searchers like me. Here was my ritual: I roamed the aisles, selecting books. In my hands, the weight of voices and stories. I was a shaggy-haired teen with only a few dollars in my pocket, but I was never hurried along. I'd find a corner and read first pages, and one by one, I returned the books to their shelves, a whittling that left me with the book I would take home.

I still have my first copy of *Slaughterhouse-Five*. The price is marked on the cover—1.50—and although I have no recollection of that day, I see myself counting change on the counter, see myself walking home in the sun or cold or rain. Forgotten or not, the moment exists, knotted into the fabric that will disappear with my death.

Forty years, and I remove the rubber bands that hold the book together. I open the cover. The taped spine crackles.

*

Biblical experts believe the destruction of Sodom and Gomorrah occurred around 2065 BC. As punishment for their wickedness, the Lord rained down fire and brimstone, destroying the city and its evil residents. Only Lot, a man deemed the sole virtuous inhabitant of Sodom, and his family were spared. The angels instructed Lot and his clan not to look back upon their burning city. When Lot's wife disobeyed, the death count increased by one.

How did Lot prove his worthiness to the angels the Lord had sent to find the righteous in Sodom? When an angry mob gathered at Lot's door, demanding the flesh of his angel visitors, he instead offered them his virgin daughters. That's how.

Sodom was burnt to cinders, but it's lived on in the word "sodomy." Prior to the 1970's, many states had sodomy laws that prohibited oral sex between married couples.

Being burnt alive often tops drowning in lists of most-feared ways to die.

*

Another list: *Slaughterhouse-Five* sits at 29th place on the American Library Association's ranking of most frequently banned books. Since its release, *Slaughterhouse-Five* has been pulled from school curriculums and library shelves. In 1972, a Michigan Circuit judge deemed the story of Billy Pilgrim "depraved, immoral, psychotic, and anti-Christian." In North Dakota, a collection of classroom copies was burned in the high-school furnace. Kurt Vonnegut, who knew a thing or two about fire and Nazis, might have been amused.

Few who've read *Slaughterhouse-Five* believe it's been attacked for its mentioning of blowjobs or baby-making. There is disgust in the book. There is, beneath the sardonic laughter, a tide disturbing and deep. Cruelty. Inhumanity. The crimes of war. The layers of human bone meal beneath a once-beautiful city. Here are the book's real obscenities.

"When I was a child, I spake as a child, I understood as a child, I thought as a child: but when I became a man, I put away childish things. For now we see through a glass, darkly; but then face to face: now I know in part; but then shall I know even as also I am known." So says First Corinthians, and here is Vonnegut's true crime—the holding close of a dark glass. He ingratiates himself with humor and a breezy voice and then slays us with truth. War is fought by children. So much is beyond us. The wheel turns, and we're ground to dust. We have been lied to, over and over again. *Slaughterhouse-Five* is un-American if being American means unquestioning obedience. It's subversive—if being subversive isn't believing one's birthright guarantees one residence in the shining city upon the hill. It's anti-Christia—if one's view of Christianity is more aligned with Sodom-leveling God of the Old Testament than with the New's gospel of love thy neighbor.

I've taught in a public high school for the past thirty-three years. I know a thing or two about learning. I've had my good days and bad. I worry about the state of the profession I still love, its hijacking by bureaucrats, its allegiance to standardized testing. We have lost the fact that not all values can be quantified and that data can't trump the nuances of perception or the gift of appreciation. Here's what I know: within ten years, 95% of current algebra students won't remember how to graph a parabola. History students will forget the details of the Compromise of 1850. They will have no idea how to calculate planetary motion. What will remain are the times that they were asked to engage in the questioning and defense that forms the framework of a compassionate mind. What they won't forget are the books and teachers who've challenged them to look in the dark glass and describe what they see.

*

And on the subject of burning books: I want to congratulate the librarians, not famous for their physical strength or their powerful political connections or their great wealth, who, all over this country, have staunchly resisted anti-democratic bullies who have tried to remove certain books from their shelves, and have refused to reveal to the thought police the names of persons who have checked out those titles.

So the America I loved still exists, if not in the White House or the Supreme Court or the Senate or the House of Representatives or the media. The America I love still exists at the front desks of public libraries.

*

By the time I graduated high school, I'd read most of Vonnegut's novels—*Mother Night, Player Piano, Cat's Cradle, Breakfast of Champions.* An English teacher noticed the titles. "So you like science fiction," he said. Thing was I didn't like science fiction, or at least I didn't like Tolkien, Heinlein, or Herbert. True, Vonnegut wrote about time travel and aliens, but his other-worldly elements paled beneath his humanity. His humor. His questioning of a society that had lost its way. His precipice-toeing view of the abyss that lurked beneath America's postwar dream. He was unafraid to shout that the emperor had no clothes, and more than any other writer of his generation, he knew how to make us wear an uncomfortable smile.

When I started this project, I retrieved my copy of

Slaughterhouse-Five from its shelf. The book had followed me over the years, packed and unpacked, a haze of a half-dozen apartments before we settled into our house. Years before the pages had come loose in chunks. Before my rereading, I took an evening to restore the book. I applied clear shipping tape to the cover. A new binding of duct-tape strips and a rejoining of the spine with super glue. Imperfect but passable. I held the cover and pulled back my thumb, a fanning of yellowed pages, a scent I hope my son will still cherish. I began to read. I underlined passages, and with the first page's tear, I employed a lighter touch. I rejoined an echo, the person I was before the deterioration of cartilage and bone, before the adult's humbling knowledge of how much was beyond me. Hello, young man, I called across the decades. Hello!

A few years ago I was rooting through our basement, and in box, I found a packet of old photographs. My early college days. Dorm life. Parties. A young me spinning a Frisbee on his finger. In the box's bottom, a glimpse of red, and I pulled out the slender notebook I hadn't held in years. Inside, the dream journal I penned as a freshman. I'd conditioned myself to wake and write, pages of bleary sentences, my penmanship a sloppy flirting with the printed lines. I sat amid the basement clutter and began to read. I was astonished how vivid the dreams were, their hues vibrant, my memory so often choked with soot and chalk. The photographs were two-dimensional proof of young faces and dated fashions, but the dreams I now revisited pulled at me, a tug in my gut. Here waited another brand of memory, one cooked up in my subconscious and played out in a code I'd never understand.

I turned another page of *Slaughterhouse-Five* and carefully penned a note in the margin. The teenager who first read these pages was gone, but he also waited, drifting, still breathing in my dreams.

*

"What if a demon were to creep after you one night, in your loneliest loneliness, and say, 'This life which you live must be lived by you once again and innumerable times more; and every pain and joy and thought and sigh must come again to you, all in the same sequence. The eternal hourglass will again and again be turned and you with it, dust of the dust!' Would you throw yourself down and gnash your teeth and curse that demon? Or would you answer, 'Never have I heard anything more divine'?"

—Friedrich Nietzsche

*

Twenty years have passed. I'm doing my best to remember, but my brain is filled with detritus, and conjured ghosts have taken the place of facts. Forgive me . . .

I am an agnostic in a beautiful church. The space majestic, high ceilings, adornments simple and modern, the stained glass dark on this mild, fall evening. Our tickets are collected at the door, and we find a spot in a pew near the back. The event sold out, the chapel's capacity a bit over five hundred. More file in, and we scoot over, making room. A hundred different conversations, a haze of voices that evaporates when the English Department Chair steps to the pulpit. Thanks are given to the endowments that have made this all possible, then the introduction.

Applause greets the guest as he rises to the microphone. I am thirty-five, the years before the blurring of my vision, and despite our distance, I see him clearly, the brown jacket and blue shirt, the unruly hair. He begins to speak, and the persona he projects—humble yet sharp, self-effacing, insightful—meshes perfectly with the voice I have come to know through the artifice of a dozen novels.

Fifty years have passed since Dresden. He talks about the firebombing and the slaughterhouse, specifics in one man's story that form a frame for a larger, sadder picture of all wars. Dresden, he contends, wasn't a tragedy. Dresden was just a turn of an endless wheel. Dresden was our horror and our fate.

Yet the mood is light. There are flowers on the altar and smiles all around. Vonnegut praises the everyday saints, the good people who behave decently in an indecent world. He confesses his secret passion for the woman who works at his local post-office window and the happiness he finds in the suddenly quaint ritual of mailing an envelope. He claims he's suing R. J. Reynolds because his beloved Pall Malls haven't killed him already. I laugh with the others even though I've heard some of this before, threads repeated from his recent essays, and I wonder if I'm listening to Kurt Vonnegut or another Billy Pilgrim.

He ends with a Q & A, but then claims the first and only question. He asks if we've ever had a teacher who's made a difference, and if so, would we please tell the person next to us their name. He thanks us, wishes us well, and says goodnight. A murmur rises in the chapel and the names of teachers are exchanged, the space filling with the memories of those who've remained with us all these years. The ones who shaped and challenged us. The ones who guided us when we were lost. My wife and I step back into the night. Cooler now, the stars crisp. I think of the wheels that turn with or without me. I think of the life within my grasp and the blessings of everyday saints.

*

Researchers at Anglia Ruskin University have been analyzing texts from ancient Mesopotamia. The accounts, which date back to 1300 BC and the early days of the Assyrian Dynasty, describe accounts of men who'd survived battle but who were then haunted by ghosts. The faces of fallen comrades. The men they'd slain.

*

The Tralfamadorians told Billy Pilgrim that one time was all time. Our flesh is a vessel, and time fills us, and when the brain's neuron storm goes dark, the liquid and flowing parts of our lives end. We are emptied, but the time we've lived is never gone. Our breathing days still exist—but only in a manner we have yet to comprehend.

The nature of time, the inevitability of death, the atrocities we so readily commit, and how we carry the memories of what we've seen—these form the novel's crux, yet they are not separate strains. Becoming unstuck in time was Billy's reflex to the nightmare of war. He tumbles heedlessly through his years. He sees his death. He can—and can't—escape his time as a soldier and prisoner. Critics have combed the pages and unearthed a number of inaccuracies in Billy Pilgrim's chronology. The years and months are sometimes skewed, the math of ages and anniversaries not adding up. Yet this is how we really perceive time, markings made with the vagaries of the heart.

On his travels through space, Billy Pilgrim asks the Tralfamadorians for something to read. Yes, they have books, but they tell Billy he wouldn't understand them. The linear spine has been removed from their novels. Their books don't contain a breadcrumb trail of clues or a convenient A-to-B trajectory. Rather, they are pools that churn with overlapping layers of events and time. The Tralfamadorians tell Billy what they love about their books "are the depths of the many marvelous moments seen all at once."

A school morning, winter dark upon the windows. The sun yet to rise. I'm knotting my tie as I roust my son. "Time to get up, bud." He's sleepy, his waking moments sluggish, payback for his night-owl ways. Years ago, we developed a ritual, the invitation of a piggyback ride to the breakfast table. I ask; he says yes. Another ritual—the offer of a countdown. "Ten seconds?" I ask. "Fifteen?"

He rubs his eyes. "Is twenty OK?"

I begin, the count altered to include his latest fascination, the history of pandemics. "Twenty . . . nineteen-eighteen was the year of the Spanish Flu . . . seventeen . . . sixteen . . . fifteen . . . fourteen . . . thirteen forty-seven was when the Black Plague hit Italy . . . twelve . . . eleven . . ."

He rises like a boxer off the canvas, covers tossed aside, and leaps onto my waiting back. He is eleven, lean yet solid. He can hold a plank longer than me. He has a knack for running, light steps and a tireless engine, and on our jogs, he's now the one now must loop back. A balance has shifted, a tide of strength destined to grow. We go down the steps. I joke that our days for such rides are numbered, that someday he may be the one carrying me. He is warm against me, his breath, his body.

We have made this trek a thousand times. Here, I understand a little more about the beauty of the Tralfamadorian novel, the wonder of wading into a past that hits all at once. This house, this stairwell, my son on my back. This indulgence. This embrace. The vision of one time as all time and a heart so full.

*

Einstein's theories revolutionized the science of time. Consider this scenario.

A clock runs on a source of regular rhythm. A pendulum's

sway. A current. A wound spring. Imagine a clock run by a ball bouncing between two plates. Each strike represents a second. The ball travels in a perfectly straight path.

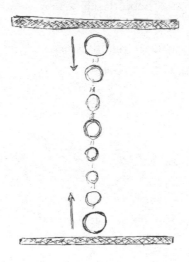

Now set this device in motion. The ball continues to bounce, but the plates are moving and so is the ball, the whole system hurtling faster and faster. The ball now moves like this—

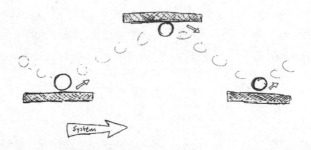

Pythagoras taught us about such distances, the hypotenuse's greater length. The ball's path stretches between plate-strikes. Speed elongates the seconds. Time expands. This is the science behind science fiction's speed-of-light narratives, the space traveler returning to an aged earth.

Time, at least theoretically, is relative, flexible. Or in the case of Billy Pilgrim, broken.

*

"We went to the New York World's Fair, saw what the past had been like, according to the Ford Motor Car Company and Walt Disney, saw what the future would be like, according to General Motors. And I asked myself about the present: how wide it was, how deep it was, how much was mine to keep."

*

In his account of the Battle of Marathon, the Greek historian Herodutus writes of Epizelus, an Athenian warrior who, despite suffering no physical injury, fell permanently blind after the soldier standing beside him was slain. Herodutus also writes of a Spartan named Aristodemus, a man so shaken by his battlefield experiences that he was given the nickname "The Trembler." Aristodemus, shamed by this un-Spartan-like betrayal of his humanity, hanged himself.

*

So it goes.

Here is *Slaughterhouse-Five*'s sad refrain, three words

that have twined their way into our language. The phrase appears over a hundred times, a period to every reference of death. The water in a glass is dead. So it goes. A hundred thousand human beings burn. So it goes. With its repetition, the saying achieves an unsettling duality, both dulling and highlighting the carnage. Billy Pilgrim adopted the saying from his interstellar abductors. The Tralfamadorians, upon seeing a corpse, viewed it not as gone forever but, in the current moment, as a body in bad condition. They claimed death was not a period but just another event in the Mobius strip of time.

The morning after the raids on Dresden, Billy Pilgrim stepped out of the slaughterhouse. I can picture the scene only as deeply as a man who hasn't seen a corpse outside a hospital or funeral service. I can fill in the background with stock footage culled from documentaries and war movies. I can call upon my limited experiences of shock, but no, I can't imagine emerging into a smoldering moonscape. I can't imagine being just a few years out of high school—a child in a children's crusade—and burying the women and children and old men that my side, the side God was supposed to be on, had killed. In this light, *So it goes* transcends a simple saying. *So it goes* is a cloak, a suit of armor, a protection against the nightmare of war and one's—no matter how distant—culpability in the deed.

Having reached my mid-fifties, I am a decade older than Kurt Vonnegut when he wrote his Dresden novel. I have buried family members and friends, but fortune has spared me the sufferings endured by so many. On Sunday mornings, I find myself looking over the obituaries, and I'm drawn to names I know—and to strangers my age or younger. The invisible hand is never far.

So it goes might offer comfort, but I don't want to be robbed of death's finality. I am twenty, maybe thirty years from my end. I cherish every day, but from this end of the continuum, I understand a lack of death would be cruel. There is beauty in a story's resolution. The years pass, and as I age, I view death as both the end and a sounding board. A relayer of echoes, of heartbeats and sighs and the steps of my march. Here is my only wish—let me keep my eyes open until I can bear to watch no more.

*

The Gospel of Matthew tells the story of Herod the Great who, fearing the Magi's prediction of the arrival of the newborn King of the Jews, ordered the death of all male children in Bethlehem. Biblical scholars refer to this as "The Massacre of the Innocents." In 1914, at the First Battle of Ypres, over 25,000 student volunteers fresh from the Fatherland's universities were cut down. The Germans named the First Ypres "Kindermord bei Ypren," the "massacre of the innocents at Ypres."

In 1645, an estimated 800,000 were slaughtered in the Yangzhou Massacre. Qing troops, under the command of Prince Dodo, conducted the killings as retribution for the city's resistance. Wang Xiuchu, an eyewitness to the massacre wrote: "The women were bound together at the necks with a heavy rope, clustered like a string of pearls, stumbling with each step, and all of their bodies covered in mud. Babies lay everywhere on the ground. The organs of those trampled like turf under horses' hooves or people's feet were smeared in the dirt, and the crying of those still alive filled the whole outdoors." The Yangzhou Massacre of 1645 shouldn't be confused with the Yangzhou Massacre of 760. Different perpetrators, different targets.

The penchant for slaughter obviously outstrips our ability to provide each with a distinct name. So it goes.

*

Consider these three theories of time and reality.

Presentism—Only that which exists now is real. The future isn't real. The past isn't real unless there is something in the present to make it true. Being alive to witness this moment is the only way to ensure something is real. Don't blink!

A Growing-Past—The present is real, of course, but so is the past, and the past grows with each second-hand tick. The future—totally unreal. Too much chaos. Too many possibilities. Who knows? Who ever knows?

Eternalism—Adherents of eternalism object to the ontological status of the past, present, or the future. Yes, they believe in the reality of these concepts, but there is no metaphysical difference between them. The delineation between past, present, and future lies in perception, a subjective classification that varies from person to person.

"Ah," say the Tralfamadorians, "now you're starting to make sense."

*

I am sixteen, and I'm spending the weekend at my brother's college. 1976 is in full swing—flared jeans, denim caps, tight shirts with colors and schemes reminiscent of mankind's hippest mode of transportation, the tricked-out van. Behind us, an afternoon of basketball in the campus gym, a trip to the cafeteria. Later, I will be adopted at a party— the youngster hanging with an increasingly rowdy crew, the room cheering me on as I crack another Pabst tallboy. Later still, after puffing my first and only clove cigarette, I will end the night kneeling on a slimy bathroom floor, a cartoonish orbit of stars around my spinning head.

But now I'm in a hall claimed by the student government for movie night. This space once the dining room in Old Main, and around us the ghosts of generations who wouldn't dream of attending dinner without a suit coat or dress. In two years, I will filter around this room, searching for department tables and amassing computer punch cards as I register for classes. In six years, I'll be here to attend my induction into Kappa Delta Pi. But all of that waits in a future that is now my past.

Folding chairs are arranged in haphazard clumps. I claim a spot near the front and sit on the floor. The 16mm projectors rest on a cart in the floor's center. The lights go out, and soon, a faint, flowery thread of smoke drifts from the bathroom. Dust motes tumble through the projector's beam. The cogs clunk and chug, the stammer of the film's shaking loop. On the screen, a scarecrow wrapped in a blanket stumbles through the snow. Here is Billy Pilgrim, lost behind enemy lines.

Hooray for the movies of the 70's, their grittiness, their antiheroes, their questioning of the American Dream. Here was my time coming up, and as a youngster, I could walk to four different theaters. In those darkened caves, surrounded by a sense of space and openness lost to today's multiplexes, I snuck in to see age-restricted fare. *The Godfather. Papillon. Dog Day Afternoon. The Conversation. Network. The Last Detail. Harry and Tonto. The Exorcist. Taxi Driver.* More.

The movie version of *Slaughterhouse-Five* was released in 1972. George Roy Hill directed. Michael Sacks played Billy Pilgrim. Valerie Perrine played Montana Wildhack. Glenn Gould, an artist whose CD I would later play nightly for my son as he drifted in his crib, performed the music. Vonnegut claimed post-war Dresden reminded him of Dayton, Ohio, and in the absence of the original, the pre-destruction Dresden scenes were shot in Prague. The film was awarded a Cannes Film Festival Jury Prize. Vonnegut, in his preface to *Between Time and Timbuktu*, called the film "a flawless translation." The sixteen year old watched, rapt by the images that, until that moment, had played only in his head.

Fast forward and thirty-eight years have passed since I watched the film's snowy opening scene. Beside me, my son.

Slaughterhouse-Five, delivered in a little red envelope, plays on our DVD. My son is a student of history, a keen observer. He knows about the Battle of the Bulge, the RAF's night raids, the Lancasters and their incendiary bombs, the target flares the Germans called Christmas trees. We settle in. We won't watch much—there is homework to do and a dog to walk. There is a nude scene I don't want him to see—but I do want him to experience the beginning. I want him to see another view of war, a perspective of what it's like to be scared and lost, a man-child with his boots full of snow.

*

In science, there are physical and chemical changes. Burning is a chemical change, a breakdown at the molecular level. Death for many burning victims comes from carbon monoxide poisoning, another type of drowning, the lungs robbed of oxygen. Victims will often suffer painful convulsions and respiratory arrest before losing consciousness. If the CO levels are lower, the victim will die of heatstroke, shock, blood loss, or the thermal decomposition of organs. Bones crack beneath the heat.

A firestorm is created when the flames grow to the point where their heat draws in the surrounding air. Small fires merge into a single, rising column. A tornado of flames. The destruction carried on gale-force winds.

The Dresden firestorm consumed eight square miles of the city. Imagine Manhattan. Now erase every building and living thing south of Central Park.

*

Nobody talked much as the expedition crossed the moon. There was nothing appropriate to say. One thing was clear: Absolutely everybody in the city was supposed to be dead, regardless of what they were, and that anybody that moved in it represented a flaw in the design. There were to be no moon men at all.

*

Lot's wife turned back, disobeying God, and for this, she was turned to a pillar of salt. As a child, I imagined this in literal of terms, an image rooted in the sensibilities of comic books. Vonnegut puts Lot's wife at the end of the first chapter. Here, he professes his love for her humanness. He tells us people aren't supposed to look back. He calls his book a failure because it was written by a pillar of salt.

Fortunately, I was allowed to grow beyond childhood, and I, too, harbor a fondness for Lot's wife. Hers wasn't an act of defiance but of fear, of shock. Of mercy. She turned back because she needed to see the horror to make it real. Perhaps I would have looked back as well. I would have needed vision's understanding. I would have needed to inventory what I'd lost before I could move ahead. I would have become another pillar of salt.

*

The Third Punic War was the last stage in the titanic struggle between Rome and Carthage over control of the Mediterranean world. The Roman commander Scipio oversaw the nearly three-year siege of Carthage. Behind the city walls, thousands starved. The final Roman onslaught killed thousands more, a house-to-house fight, the streets running red. The 50,000 Carthaginians who survived were either slaughtered or sold into slavery. The Romans then systematically burned the city. Legend contends Scipio ordered the land sown with salt so nothing would grow there ever again.

*

A memory—I'm a college freshman. Behind the art building, blackened letters stretch across the lawn. I step closer and smile. The message: SALT BURNS GRASS.

Perhaps Lot's wife lived, but inside, she was filled with salt, burned and hollowed and dead.

*

In 1908, John McTaggart published his influential essay "The Unreality of Time." He proposed two ways of considering time—the A-series and B-series. A-theorists believe in the concept of presentism or, to a degree, the growing past. The A's ask one to picture time as a continual parade of past, present, and future—a world as thoroughly tensed as our language—was, is, and will be. An event was once in the unknowable future passes through the tangible and real present. It slips into the past, a process that causes it to both disappear and become forever preserved. To the A-crowd, what matters is the objective now. Only in the present can we flex our muscles. Only in the present can we be kind. Only in the present can we create art or make love. Only in the present can we alter our world.

McTaggart's B-theory runs on a simpler language. In their embrace of eternalism, the B's have abandoned those pesky verb tenses. Time, they contend, is a man-made scaffolding which allows the assignment of order to the orderless. It is an invention, just like the wheel or lever, a tool that has served us well, but still an artificial conceit. The only flow time possesses is that which we see in our thoughts. Past, present, and future are real—all at once, right now—just as they have been since man's first flicker of awareness.

Unlike Billy Pilgrim, the B-theorists just might enjoy checking out a few Tralfamadorian novels.

*

"The distinction between past, present, and future is only a stubbornly persistent illusion." —Albert Einstein

*

We go to the beach in the summers we don't have a major expense—a new car, a dead furnace. A few days, the sea air, the sun. The cool sting of outdoor showers. We absorb ourselves in the rhythms and entertain the lazy dream of staying all year, but the notion is fleeting. I'm a woods person, and I would miss my hills and trees and the windings of rocky paths. A ritual—a final walk along the beach. The car packed, the rental property cleaned. Ahead, the drive home. The traffic. The aspirin I'll take to appease my aching back.

My wife and son and I watch the waves. Their width, their endless march. The surf fans across the sloped shore, and beneath the foam, a tumbling of pebbles and broken shells. My footprints disappear beneath the next push. Not so long ago, I didn't enjoy the beach. I was fidgety, unable to find comfort. My mind raced—the calling of tasks and projects, the outsider's dissonance in my thoughts, the connection that came easily to others lost on me. This perspective, like so many others, changed with my son. I found my place holding his hand at the continent's edge. Together, we ventured into the breakers, and when he gathered his courage, he let go of my hand. Down he'd go, sometimes lost beneath water as gray as concrete, before popping up. My heart spiked, then settled until his next tumble.

Another perspective shift—the losing of my fear of water. In my late thirties, I learned to swim, and with a new confidence, I ventured beyond the breakers. The shelf dropped, and I bobbed upon the swells, enjoying a calm I hadn't expected, my thoughts singular and blissfully focused on nothing beyond the next wave and the decision to rise with the crest or ride to the shore. I stayed until my son waved me in or I grew too tired or cold. Dripping, I walked the wet sand, the ocean's rhythm still in me, shivers in my muscles. I lay on my towel. The warmth returned. I listened to the waves, the umbrellas' breeze-whipped canvas, the gulls, and I found myself thankful for the gift of change, the gift of having another year to understand what I hadn't before.

My son tosses a final shell into the waves. We've walked farther than I'd imagined, the lifeguard posts and beach umbrellas toying with my perspective. A gull hovers, motionless on the breeze. A little girl lowers a pink bucket into the surf. The waves roll in, break, retreat. We'll return next year or the year after that. My son will be taller, stronger, and if I'm fortunate, I will have faded in all the expected ways. We will return, again and again. Then will come the summer I am gone.

Hello. Farewell. Hello. Farewell. This is what the waves sing. Billy Pilgrim echoes this Tralfamadorian saying before he's struck by an assassin's bullet. Hello, farewell—as steady as my pulse, and here is the rhythm of our days. The hellos of reunion, the first glimpses of the newborns and lovers who will fill our hearts. The farewells that bring tears and the empty spaces never to be filled.

It's time to go. From atop the dunes, we turn for a final look. The wide vista. The long lines of breakers. The horizon's kiss of sea and sky. Hello. Farewell. Hello.

*

"And Nietzsche, with his theory of eternal recurrence. He said that the life we lived we're going to live over again the exact same way for eternity. Great. That means I'll have to sit through the Ice Capades again."   —Woody Allen

*

Not so long ago our world was full of time travelers!

A person riding the transcontinental railroad in the 1870's

would, if they cared to be in synch with their surroundings, have to adjust their pocket watch hundreds of times. A minute forward here, three back there, each county and city keepers of their own official clock. This lackadaisical attitude didn't sit well with Cornelius Vanderbilt and the other railroad barons, their empires built on making connections and the shipment of goods. On November 18, 1883, time zones were established across the United States, and the following year, at an international gathering in Washington DC, the world was segmented into twenty-four time zones. Welcome globalization!

The businessmen of the world set their clocks accordingly. The tribesmen of the vanishing wilderness turned their eyes to the sun, just as their ancestors had.

*

The end of the 1950's saw Vonnegut at a pivotal point of his career. He'd already put out *Player Piano*, was about to publish *Sirens of Titan*, and was in the midst of his long struggle with *Cat's Cradle*. He'd made decent money from his stories, the heady days of *Colliers* and *Saturday Evening Post* and a half dozen other magazines that could keep a writer with a young family afloat, if not rich. He was penning plays and enjoying the process, but his theater work hadn't received the recognition he'd hoped. He dabbled in movie scripts, sculpture. He pitched a military-themed board game to uninterested toy companies. He took a teaching job with troubled boys but quit after a semester. He claimed he struggled with writer's block, but his work kept coming. Perhaps his condition just felt like writer's block, his Dresden book still inside, pushing, gnawing, waiting to take form.

In a 1959 letter to Knox Burger, an early publisher of Vonnegut's stories and longtime mentor and friend, Vonnegut wrote: "And tell me—when one is being frog-marched by life, does one giggle or does one try to maintain as much dignity as possible under the circumstances?"

I've got to believe Kurt Vonnegut already knew the answer. I see it written in *Player Piano* and *Sirens of Titan* and the stories he'd already published. And I see it waiting in *Cat's Cradle*, *Slaughterhouse-Five*, *Breakfast of Champions*, *Bluebeard*, and a dozen others. Kurt Vonnegut believed in the dignity of laughter. Laughter, if not our most human gift, then a close second behind kindness and/or the magic of baby-making. Laughter made his characters walk a little taller. Laughter, like dignity, arose from courage, from looking one's fears dead in the eye.

And "frog-marched"—one's arms pinned behind one's back, a convict's walk and a rousting by greater powers. "Frog-marched by life"—how true. How sad and funny and true.

*

A beautiful afternoon, early November, autumn's pale sky. We climb the church steps. On the entrance overhang, a gray statue, Saint Joan, her head bowed, her hands resting upon her sword's pommel. Only a few inside, the space hushed and cavernous. My wife and son cross themselves. We pass slender columns of stained glass. Yesterday was my father's birthday, our plans to come derailed by homework and a chance to sneak in a jog before the weekend's projected cold snap. Last month we found my son in tears, sad because he both missed his grandfather and because he feared he'd soon no longer be able to remember the old man he'd loved so much. We've had this conversation before—how much joy my son brought to my father's life, his last years enriched by this new relationship, how memories fade but also leave us with something deeper, a residue of the love we've given and shared—but for my son, the sense of grief seems set on an odd cycle, an emerging untethered to the logic of clocks and calendars. My father is, after all, the first person my son has lost.

We allow my son to light one of the few unclaimed candles. Flames burn in slender glasses, Veterans Day, a remembering of soldiers gone, and from the candles' tiered racks, a heat I hadn't anticipated. My son writes in the prayer book. My father's name, a set of dates, *US Army*. We slide into a nearby pew. I'm not a religious man, yet I admire the faith that drives charity and brotherhood. I appreciate the beauty and security to be found in ritual, and as I kneel beside my family in this beautiful prism of stillness and colored light, I wonder if I should accept the story of a man sent to spread a message of love, not literally but as a veil that drapes a current so often covered beneath the spill of blood. I rise and settle into the pew. My son remains kneeling.

Vonnegut wasn't a religious man, either. He was a humanist, an avowed free thinker. Yet a profound strain of compassion runs through his work, a foundation of empathy worthy of Jesus or any other benevolent deity. In *The Sirens of Titan* he writes, "A purpose of a human life, no matter who is controlling it, is to love whoever is around to be loved." Here's a quote that could just as easily come from the New Testament than from a novel about interplanetary invasion. Consider Billy Pilgrim. He is human, yes, but also a messenger from another world. He sleeps standing in the boxcar on the way to the POW camp, his arms outstretched to support himself, an outcast even among his sorry fellow travelers. He has walked through the garden and the wasteland. He is a martyr, his death preordained, a note in a larger scheme. Through his letters to newspapers, radio appearances, and speeches, he brings the world good news meant to ease death's sting.

I too think about death, and without religion or the insight of extraterrestrials, I have no creed to soothe the trepidation that unknowing brings. I'd like to think I'm not afraid, but such statements come easily to a healthy man. Perhaps I will find God, perhaps not. Either way, I will stumble forward, making mistakes but trying not to make the same ones twice.

My wife and son rise, and together, the three of us exit the church. We have another hour of daylight. I'm happy to be here, to love these people who are around to be loved. We walk down the street, and I rest my hand upon my son's shoulder. How, I wonder, will he remember all of this?

*

If I should ever die, God forbid, I hope you will say, "Kurt is up in heaven now." That's my favorite joke.

*

A cool Sunday, and my son and I ascend a steep passage along the Appalachian Trail. The leaves just past peak, and around us, the season's grays and browns. Up we go, a switchback trail, the path narrow in spots, a drop off to one side, the empty air and the upper branches of trees. My son forges ahead. We've been hiking since he could walk, and I'm thankful for the gift of health that allows him to take the lead. Late fall and the hint of looming winter, the hush and the muted tones—here is my favorite time of year. The chill upon my face and the kindled heat beneath my jacket. An hour's climb, the grade steep in spots, stones that serve as stairs. We reach the summit, a nub in a thousand-mile ridge, and rest upon a boulder larger than our house. The valley opens before us, the road we drove earlier a gray thread, the wide Susquehanna beyond, and above, circling hawks.

The Tralfamadorians chided Billy Pilgrim for his earthling's habit of asking *why*. There was no *why*, they said. There simply *is*. Perhaps the Tralfamadorians were right. Perhaps *why* is a human luxury, an appropriation of brainpower freed from the caveman's wiring of fight or flight. For much of my life I had difficulty enjoying myself. I could smile and laugh, but beneath, I often lapsed into contemplation. I wondered if I was truly happy or simply wearing its mask—and if I was happy, what were the components of happiness? How did happiness work? It took me years to understand that the happiness I yearned for wouldn't be found at a party or a bar. The happiness I would cherish would be intimate. Solitary. Give me a blank page and a pen. Give me a hand to hold. Give me a trail to walk with my son. Give me the struggle of trying to comprehend what speaks to me. *Why?* I ask. *Why?*

Sometimes I wish I could read a cherished book again for the first time. The surprise, the freshness, the audacity of language, the beauty of making connections—they would once more be mine to experience. The first time I read *Slaughterhouse-Five* I had yet to kiss a girl. I had yet to suffer the loss of a loved one. The fifteen-year-old believed that through the sheer act of being, he would make the world sit up and notice. Today I am older. Humbled. Grateful to simply count myself among the living.

I shiver in the unblocked wind. My son has his own questions today, and we talk about whatever he likes. We sit upon the cold rocks. The two of us part of this beautiful scene. The two of us asking why.

*

"Time is the longest distance between two places."

—Tennessee Williams

*

ABOVE YOU THE STEPS OF GIANTS THE TREM-
BLING EARTH YOU IN ITS BOWELS AND HOW
CONVENIENT THAT YOU'VE LINED YOURSELF IN
THIS TOMB YOUR HANDS OVER YOUR HEAD A
RAIN OF PLASTER AND PAINT AND WHAT GOOD
WOULD YOUR HUDDLED POSE DO IF THE CEIL-
ING CAVED THE TONS OF EARTH YOUR BURI-
AL COMPLETE BUT YOU HOLD THE POSE AN
ABSURD REFLEX AS IF YOU HAVE ANY SAY-SO IN
THIS NIGHTMARE AND THE SHAKING CONTIN-
UES THE GIANTS ON THE MARCH THEIR STEPS
NEAR THEN FAR THEN NEAR AGAIN AND YOU'RE
TRAPPED IN THIS HOLLOW SPACE AND WITHIN
YOU AN ECHOING OF OTHER HOLLOW SPACES
PRIVATE SPACES AND NO ONE SLEEPS AND WHEN
THE BARRAGE HALTS YOU GUESS IT'S DAWN
ALTHOUGH YOU CAN'T BE SURE

*

I stand along the creek's edge. A fifty-yard reach to the
opposite shore, these past two days of rain. Silt and smooth
stones underfoot, the white dotting of Asiatic clams. The
shoreline with its curves and hollows. The fishermen's
trash. A length of gnarled siding wrapped around a tree, a

reminder of last autumn's floods. I throw stones, the Osages' green balls. The current swift, my offerings short-lived. A splash. Gone.

Billy Pilgrim, through his interactions with benevolent aliens, came to see human life as liquid, a flowing state. To die is to stop flowing. So it goes. The greater stream flows on, and the droplets that evaporate into the atmosphere and the splashes that wash the shore mean nothing. The communal tide that claims us today flows on, and in its churning, part of us must remain. All those years of collisions and jostlings. The love and fights and kindnesses shared. The echoes of this kinetic dance.

The laws of chemistry state that matter can neither be created nor destroyed, and in this light, can a moment—a moment made of all that is concrete and tangible—really disappear? Perhaps this living second is another form of matter, at least in the deeply racked focus of the fourth dimension. Shift from the chemist to the physicist. He needs the past to exist; without its anchor, his attempts to calculate velocity and acceleration, growth and decay, would float off, lost in a world that couldn't lay claim to its past.

I leave the water and make my way back to the trail. The flow behind me and within.

*

In 1937, between 9,000 and 20,000 Haitian Creoles were killed on the order of the Dominican dictator Rafael Trajillo. The murders were brutal—machetes and clubs.

Men, women, children. Many bodies were cast into the Massacre River, a waterway named after an earlier ugliness between the Spanish and French. The bodies, bloated as the days passed, flowed to the sea.

How did two tribes who shared the same sunny island tell each other apart? Dominican solders were said to have carried sprigs of parsley and then ask suspected Haitian Creoles to pronounce its Spanish name, "perejil." Those whose first language was Creole had difficulty saying the word, a fault of translation and phonics. Those who failed were cut down along with their families.

History has christened it "The Parsley Massacre."

*

"Those who can make you believe absurdities, can make you commit atrocities." —Voltaire

*

I am twenty-five. It's been a night of poor decisions, and now it's after midnight, summer rain on the fields. Every so often, a lightning flash, white tendrils hotter than the sun, moments of illumination and then darkness again. The road, black and slick, disappears beneath our rushing headlights. My friend is in no condition to drive, but neither am I. Wind whips through the windows. We laugh at nothing, the stereo too loud. We come upon a sharp turn, a dogleg that no doubt dates back generations, a boundary between farms, a cattle path long paved over. We're going too fast, the road too wet, and the truth of physics is born out—velocity, friction, deceleration, centripetal motion, our car turning then spinning. I see a farmhouse and barn, a swirling of dark pastures and distant lights.

We slide off the road, backend first, and not two feet from my window, a wide-trunked oak, close enough to touch, to smell. We come to a stop. My heart pounds. Our laughter is a reflex of shock and the starshine of adrenaline.

In the first chapter of *Slaughterhouse-Five*, Vonnegut and his war buddy Bernard O'Hare return to Dresden. There, they befriend a local taxi driver, a man whose mother was incinerated in the firestorm. The following Christmas, the taxi driver sends O'Hare a postcard that ends with: "I hope that we'll meet again in a world of peace and freedom in the taxicab if the accident will."

If the accident will. Free will, that earthly concept that so perplexed the Tralfamadorians, is our gift, but free will's power dwindles beside the impact of accidents. If the accident will our cell cycles won't turn upon us and generate the tumor that spells the beginning of the end. If the accident will the lockdowns at our children's schools will only be drills. If the accident will the trees our cars skid by won't slam against our skulls, our brains scrambled and darkness forever. If the accident will—and I think of the separated-at-birth twins reunited as gray adults, the traveler who missed his flight on the airplane that went down in flames. So much depends upon if the accident will.

I look back, five decades, and as Billy Pilgrim's mother asked, "How did I get so old?" The years stretch behind me, my memories fading at a rate beyond the quantifying powers of mathematicians. I have lived one life, and in each moment, I have made one decision, and thus, from the vantage point of a man closer to death than he'd like to admit, my days appear as single path. There are turns, yes, loops and double-backs, yet my perception of the fourth dimension constricts me from seeing it otherwise.

Consider our actions, our actual physical doings, as a kind of electric charge. String these together and behold the arc of our lives, a lightning bolt across the sky, yet beneath this illuminated heartbeat there exist a million filaments left dark, the branching nexus of choices unmade, the routes untraveled. All is not the will of accidents, yet so much is accidental, and another image comes to mind, the popular game of pachinko, which in this context, might look like this—

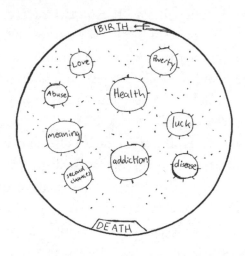

*

Famous accidental discoveries—Velcro, Viagra, dynamite, the Slinky, LSD, Teflon, the X-ray, the microwave, corn flakes.

*

Listen to the Tralfamadorian advise Billy Pilgrim on the nature of human suffering: "Ignore the awful times and concentrate on the good ones." The message is seductive, its peace, its acceptance. The words flow, a simple mantra, a balm no different than man's other balms. His religions. His delusions and distractions. His powders and spirits.

I also enjoy pretty things, but I can't look at them all the time. Neither does Vonnegut. Consider all the pretty things he offers for our viewing. The corpse mines of Dresden. The candles made from the fat of slaughtered Jews. The dead eyes of Russian prisoners. Billy's breakdowns, his estrangement from his children. The Tralfamadorians, with their passivity and denial of free will, bring us a mindset every bit as culpable as the Nazis and Bomber Command and all the other bearers of self-justified horror, all of them cousins in groupthink and willful blindness. In total war, one's enemies sink to the subhuman. They are vermin, worthy only of extermination. The Tralfamadorians, beyond hate yet caught in their shallow realm of pretty things, are simply indifferent. Perpetrator or bystander—either way, the butchery continues.

So give me my pretty things, but don't withhold the sad. Give me the sorrows that will help me savor the days when all is well. Give me the miseries that will break me with the sting of melancholy. Give me the beauty only a heavy heart can understand. And if the accident will, let me be strong enough to see another day.

*

In 1678, Dr. Johannes Hofer was treating Swiss mercenaries who'd returned from their wars, and in his rounds, he noted a number who suffered symptoms including depression, insomnia, loss of appetite, anxiety, heart palpitations, and stupor. Combining the Greek roots *nostos* (homecoming) and *algos* (pain), he coined their affliction *nostalgia*, the pain of coming home. In 1761, Austrian physician Josef Leopold Auenbrugger noted in his book *Invetun Novum* that he'd worked with soldiers who'd "become sad, taciturn, listless, solitary, musing, full of sighs and moans . . . this disease is called *nostalgia*."

The use of the term has evolved, its meaning kinder, an affliction perceived as more sweet than bitter, a revisiting that has filtered out the unpleasant. The Tralfamadorians would approve of this selective memory, yet another pull runs beneath these sunny recollections. The nostalgia of today is a self-serving narrative. My generation grows nostalgic for their childhood, forgetting segregation and sexism and Cold-War fears. The Tralfamadorians, who'd urged Billy Pilgrim to focus only on the good, have replaced memory with nostalgia. Happiness is theirs but not truth.

*

Ancient Egyptians viewed history and cosmology as structured and cyclical. Man-made changes, no matter how radical, were viewed as inconsequential variations from the Gods' plans or as part of the plans' necessary transformation. Thus, the relevance of the present was merely a single step in a long, cosmic journey. To the ancient Egyptians, death wasn't an end but a transition in existence's flow, and the tombs of the powerful often contained sacrificed servants to tend to their masters in the next world. This arrangement comforted the powerful in their final days. Their servants, not so much.

*

When I was five, I refused to leave the house without my holster and silver cap gun. I don't remember this, but my mother says it's the truth, and she has the photographs to prove it. There I am, chin lifted, squinting, revolver in hand, my father's shadow extending beside me. The pose doesn't surprise me for I was a child fascinated by war. I was drawn to one of our house's prize possessions—a set of green-covered encyclopedias, their illustrations, their glossy pages, their histories of battles and campaigns. Outside, my friends and I acted out scenarios of death and valor, running battles in the alley, and if a toy gun wasn't available, I imagined one in my grasp, its barrel aimed at another little boy's heart. I was also a child who enjoyed his time alone, and many days, I ignored the sunlight to play inside with my army men. I owned different sets. Napoleonic horsemen. Civil War men in gray and blue. Cowboys and Indians. World War II Germans and Americans. Modern soldiers who held M-16s, the kind of rifle I saw boys carrying nightly on the TV news. Each set had its standard poses, the rifle-pointing soldiers I aligned in neat arrays. Yet each also had a special, singular piece, a figure I'd arrange with extra care as I wove his silent history, a man just shot, his hands outstretched or clutching his chest. A man on the brink of death.

In the first chapter of *Slaughterhouse-Five*, Vonnegut reunites with his war buddy, Bernard O'Hare. The men talk as their children play upstairs, but Vonnegut receives an icy welcome from O'Hare's wife, Mary. Finally she unleashes, accusing Vonnegut of wanting to write a book that will only romanticize war: "You'll be played in the movies by Frank Sinatra and John Wayne or some other glamorous war-loving, dirty old men. And war will look just wonderful, so we'll have a lot more of them. And they'll be fought by babies." Vonnegut wins her over with his promise to name his book *The Children's Crusade*, which eventually became part of the novel's rather lengthy subtitle.

The theme of soldier-as-child is repeated throughout the text. When I first read it, I didn't understand this reference as I do now. In my late teens, I considered myself a man. I was strong. I believed in my own invincibility. Now I understand I was a man, but only in the most superficial and rudimentary of ways.

A child imagines the world in basic hues. There is good and bad, and the only pain youngsters can truly appreciate is the pain they've experienced. A child grows, and the complexity of thought fragments what were once easy truths. June 1969, and the boy who possessed a starry-eyed notion of war thumbed through the just-arrived issue of *LIFE* magazine, a weekly highlight of those years. A special issue, page after page of service photos of the 242 Americans killed in a recent week in Vietnam. I was used to the TV's weekly casualty reports. Those were just numbers, abstractions, but here were names. Here were faces. White boys and black, kids who looked like my brother and his friends. The ones who sometimes shot basketball with us, the laughing giants we swarmed, all of us thrilled to be playing against older boys.

I began to realize war was about humans, boys and young men, the strongest offered for slaughter. Increasingly I understood war was also about death beyond the pitch of battle. The innocents caught in the crossfire. The villagers running down a dirt road, their huts ablaze. Then I read *Slaughterhouse-Five*, and my focus cut deeper. I saw war's confusion. Its absurdity. Its millions of babies given sharp sticks and cast into a hell of burning cities. I saw war through the eyes of Billy Pilgrim, an innocent on the verge of death, a soldier not making a heroic stand but hallucinating, his shoes full of snow.

Like father, like son, and here is my boy on the cusp of twelve. He has his own fascination with war, and while I had a set of encyclopedias, he's grown up with the Internet and cable TV, his storehouse of facts infinitely richer than mine.

His pacifist parents have indulged him with toy firearms and road trips to see battleships and tanks. But there is a facet of knowledge that was mine which my son will not experience: when I attended Vonnegut's lecture, the First Gulf War was a recent memory, and Vonnegut lamented the coverage Americans were receiving, the images shot by cameras high in the sky, the video-game graphics that put a pleasing veneer on the dying being done below. Together, the Pentagon and the White House had imposed restrictions on battlefield reporting, and my boy will grow up seeing war as a child setting up Army men does—removed, cartoonish, his enemies reduced to cutout figures robbed of their humanity. Lot's wife was punished for looking back on her burning city, but we, in our supposedly free society, have gone a step further, our perspective hemmed by the blinders we are only too willing to wear.

The government argued such efforts were intended to protect the privacy of soldiers and their families, a noble guise that masked their desire to sanitize the butchery, an adman's quest to sell us a product of a bloodless war. Consider the case of Tami Silicio. During the Second Gulf War, as an employee of government-contracted Maytag Aircraft, she was fired after a photo she'd taken of flag-draped coffins appeared in the *Seattle Times*. Here was an image—anonymous, respectful, its gore hidden beneath closed lids—our government didn't want us to see. The first-hand realities of war are already obscured by a volunteer army underrepresented by the middle and privileged classes.

Now we are denied the second-hand visuals that could help us see our wars in more human terms. The Tralfamadorians would nod their hand-shaped heads in approval.

On my way through the living room, I pick up a plastic rifle and here is my challenge—to guide my son's vision, to introduce him to the reality of war while sparing him its testimony to the sickness that coils in our collective hearts.

Is this even possible?

*

Much of the Children's Crusade has been lost to history. The Fourth Crusade ended in disaster in 1204. In the years soon following, separate movements arose in France and Germany, each led by a charismatic boy who claimed he had received instructions from Christ to return to the Holy Lands. They would be armed not with swords but with the Word of God. These groups gathered followers as they toured the countryside, the flock believing when they reached the Mediterranean, the waters would open and they'd walk to Jerusalem. An estimated 30,000 reached the port cities, and when the sea failed to part, they boarded seven boats. None of them reached the Holy Lands. They drowned when their boats sank; the survivors sold into slavery.

However one small contingent arrived at Genoa and found no ships awaiting them. The locals fed and sheltered the children then urged them to return to their villages. As Mary O'Hare said, "Hooray for the good people of Genoa."

*

"But Jesus said, Suffer the little children, and forbid them not, to come unto me; for such is the kingdom of heaven."
—Matthew 19:14

*

The doctors of post-Renaissance Europe struggled to name the afflictions they noted in men returning from war. The Germans came up with *heimweh* and the French with *maladie du pays*, both of which can loosely be translated into "homesickness." The Spanish coined *estar roto*, which means simply, "to be broken."

*

I spend an afternoon teaching at a retreat in Philadelphia. A room too warm, and in me, the fatigue born of words weighed and judged before they're spoken. Am I being kind? Encouraging? Clear? The sessions end and after our goodbyes, I start the drive home. There is the morning's direct route, but the clear skies and promise of a few more hours of daylight convince me to take a different way. The roads soon become familiar, and I begin to anticipate my turns, a reflex of memory. There is change, new stores, landmarks gone, yet much is the same, these little yards and tightly packed houses. I'm taken back, a journey of body and years, and finally, I park.

There is homecoming. Then there's homecoming to the home that no longer exists. I get out and walk. The street runs narrow, the parking tight. I won't stay long. Thirty-seven years have passed since I lived here, and in my thoughts, another layer, the novella waiting on my desk, a similar scene, a broken man's return to the place where he was last an innocent. As I wrote, I immersed myself with memories of this street, and today, the real me walks beside the fictive me. Here is the porch where we played step-ball. There is the curb where we groped beneath parked cars after the balls had sailed over our heads.

A heavier thump finds my heart. Steam from my mouth, the cracked sidewalk beneath my boots, and between my head and toes, a ghost who's lost his claim to this place. I pass homes I once knew, their features softened by the growth of shrubs and my fading memory. Here is nostalgia's less welcome current, the dissonance of forgetting, the white hum that replaces memory.

I consider the house where I grew up. I imagine its narrow stairwell, the tiny bedrooms that grew so hot in the summer. Billy Pilgrim travels back to his Indiana boyhood. My character collapses in his old front yard. I'm not a bug in amber. Time has passed. I have aged. My neighbors have moved or died. I have traded innocence for knowledge, as the world demands. Our houses turn to shells. We lose what is precious, but if we're lucky, we find it again, in the proximity of our children, in the quiet of a new house where all—at least for today—is OK.

I leave, a final glimpse as I drive by. Four lanes of Haverford Avenue wait at the block's end. I turn and pick up speed. Haverford Avenue, the Schuylkill Expressway, the turnpike west. The flow absorbs me. I'm going home.

*

A week later, I dream about this same block. In the dream, I am with my wife and son. All is opposite. We approach from the street's other end, the day warm and blue, the gardens bright with flowers. There is the familiar—or what I convince myself is familiar—but then the street narrows into a bar, and where my house once stood are now tables. Just beyond, the street continues. I ask the hostess and am told the house that had once stood here was torn down years ago. A struggle begins, not of bodies but of consciousness, and I try to tell her I was just here. Things had changed but not like this. I open my mouth, but my words are drowned by the bar's clamor.

*

Life is a journey.
Death is a return to earth.
The universe is like an inn.
The passing years are like dust.

Regard this phantom world
As a star at dawn, a bubble in a stream,
A flash of lightning in a summer cloud,
A flickering lamp—a phantom—and a dream.
—Gautama Buddha

*

Count the times we are presented with Adam and Eve in *Slaughterhouse-Five*. Billy half-frozen behind enemy lines, laughing, lost in body and mind as he endures a beating by the sadistic Roland Weary. Then their capture, and in the lovingly shined boots of a German officer—a pair of boots pried from a dead man's feet—Billy sees the radiant image of Adam and Eve. We meet Adam and Eve again at the end of a backward movie, a film that plays in Billy's mind alone, an unzipping of narrative and suffering, a rolling back to the Garden. A time before sin. Beneath the dome of their Tralfamadorian zoo, Billy becomes Adam and the lovely Montana Wildhack becomes his Eve. They attain love, closeness, a child—but their happiness is a lobotomized bliss. Outside the dome, an atmosphere of cyanide, their free will traded for security. A world empty of temptation.

Billy is called back to the garden in his own life. Listen: the Nazis lead Billy and the other naked POWs into a long, tiled room lined with showerheads but no faucets. An unseen hand turns a valve, a scene repeated with grimmer results elsewhere in the Reich. Hot rain pours out, thawing Billy's frozen body, and he travels to his infancy, a baby pulled from the bath, a room rosy and sunny. His cooing mother dries him, her touch gentle on his smooth skin. Here was his innocence, his imagined paradise. We, Vonnegut's readers, understand the dream's lure. It's tempting to think we once knew a time when all was well and right. Then the years, the flow. Greater forces steered us. Our pets died, then our grandparents, and each year the desert around us grew. The world didn't change—we did, as we must. The garden exists, but only in our minds. We join Lot's wife, looking back, wanting to understand what we've lost.

Adam and Eve are made tragic by their humanity. The fall appeals to us, for while we can't comprehend happiness unending, we can relate to the pull of desire, to the pain of failure and lost faith. We know Adam and Eve not through the idyllic days in the Garden but in the bite of the apple. In the expulsion from paradise.

Yet paradise exists—not as a destination or a rolling continent—but as the occasional scene waiting along the riverside. We flow past, and if the fog lifts, if the current isn't too swift, if we can abandon our struggle to keep our heads above water for one, lonely second, we can turn our gaze upon the shore. A glimpse, that's all we need. A scent. If we're lucky, we recognize the moment and bask in its goodness. We think along the lines of Vonnegut's favorite uncle and echo his words:

"If this isn't nice, I don't know what is."

*

The Gospel of Kilgore Trout

And so it came to pass that a tree unlike any other rose from the great plane. And its flowers bloomed not with nectar but with the bonds bearing the seal of the kingdom's treasury. And the fruit it begat were diamonds more pure than any of the king's mine, and lo, the sun shone upon the fruit and the light blinded the eyes of the pilgrims who came to behold this wonder. And the leaves of the tree were pale green, each baring the face of the dead king who had proven his might on the battlefield, and lo, when the great wind blew off the plane, the leaves did dance, and the pilgrims swore the dead king did smile upon them.

And the word spread across the land, and an exodus formed, and the men and women and children came from every quarter to behold the tree and pick of its fruits. But lo, beneath the tree's spreading branches the multitudes did struggle, and much wickedness was done in the battle, and great was the bloodshed and suffering, and the gore piled deep as the hands of the many reached in vain to the tree's gifts.

And the tree grew stronger and higher by the year, and its roots fed upon the blood and bone and tears of the many, and their cry lifted, a wind born from the carnage of this earth and the leaves of the mighty tree did stir as if they were gripped by laughter.

*

The bell rings, and the hallways clear. A locker slams. A boy jogs past. At the hallway's end, a couple's goodbye kiss. I stand at the juncture of two hallways, a bit of supervision in the between-class maw. On the way back to my room, I stoop to pick up a plastic water bottle.

I'm not perfect in this practice of good citizenship. If I were running late or in a funk, I might pass over a piece of trash. I won't pick up anything damp or bloody or half eaten. I rise, a deliberate straightening, wary of the stabbing that sometimes buckles my knee, wary of the too-quick movement that can leave me dizzy, spots dancing before my eyes.

In the days before the destruction of Dresden, Billy Pilgrim and the other prisoners were visited by Howard W. Campbell, an American-born Nazi who'd come to recruit his ex-countrymen to join the Germans in their fight against Communism. The POWs were given a decision. They could stay put. Or they could join Campbell and receive new uniforms and decent food and a chance to fight the real enemy, the Godless communists. Campbell, like Kilgore Trout and Eliot Rosewater, is one of Vonnegut's literary transients, a character who surfaces in a number of novels. Campbell owns center stage in *Mother Night,* and it's here we find a quote that best summarizes him—and perhaps the rest of us. "We are what we pretend to be, so we must be careful about what we pretend to be."

When I pick up a hallway scrap, I think of an old friend, a teacher I admired, a man gone too soon. From him, I took this silent cue, a gesture that added not to the man I was but to the one I wanted to be. My generation was urged to be true to one's self, but what is self but an endless performance, a high-wire act of a hundred daily choices, a juggling of forces and desires. There is much to admire about Billy Pilgrim. He is kind. He doesn't raise his voice. He doesn't complain. He doesn't add to the war's carnage. He is a loving husband. But look at him in another light, and his all-accepting peace rubs against the notion of the ever-evolving self. Like Billy Pilgrim, I want to be good, but being good isn't a passive engagement. Being good is a struggle, a daily performance. I drop the bottle in a recycling bin. I think of my friend and thank him for helping me better understand my role.

*

The Massacre of Latins occurred in Constantinople in 1182. The local Greek Orthodox population, spurred by motives of economics, class, and religion, killed between 60,000 and 80,000 Catholics. Historians report the slaughter quickly expanded beyond the Italian merchants to include children and the hospitals' bed-ridden patients. The severed head of Cardinal John, the city's papal legate, was tied to a dog's tail and dragged through the streets.

Not to be outdone, the Catholics demonstrated their own mob-violence chops when they targeted the Huguenots in 1572 in the St. Bartholomew's Day Massacre. Between 5,000 and 30,000 Huguenots were cut down in Paris, this on the eve of a royal wedding when many of France's most prominent Huguenot families had traveled to the capital to celebrate. It's said that upon learning of the slaughter, Phillip II of Spain laughed for the only time on record.

*

"Even if God is dead, you're still going to kiss his ass."
—Tony Soprano

*

I possess a morbid fascination with World War I. Its futility. The boredom and horror of the trenches. The twilight of chivalry and the dawn of mechanized carnage. My grandfather owned a book that both frightened and called me, *A Pictorial History of The Great War* (because who, at the time of its printing, would have guessed it was only act one in a greater, bloodier passion?). The book was oversized and thick, page after page of soldiers cowering beneath hails of steel. Bloated bodies. Men in field hospitals missing arms and legs, jaws and noses. Victors standing over corpse piles. Generals in their pomp and regalia, their dress hats stacked high with feathers and frills. Archduke Ferdinand's blood-stained uniform. One image haunted me more than the others—a photo of a half-naked man with dull, penetrating eyes. Beneath, the caption: *A Victim of Shell Shock.*

Fourth and fifth grade—and with lights out, the fear would creep over me. I believed in the swirl of malevolent currents. Violence. Death. A network of evil that operated just out of sight. I saw it on the news. I read it in the afternoon paper. Some nights the dread hung so heavy that I lay paralyzed, my heart a wild thing, my breathing shallow and rapid. Images drifted through the moonlight, and in the shadows, a man there but not. A face I recognized, a horror I couldn't know. A victim of shellshock.

Stupid, thought the adolescent who no longer saw the ghosts, but forty years has softened my judgment of that frightened boy. Tonight, I think of Billy Pilgrim. And I think of the picture in my grandfather's book. Two more children in a children's crusade. And I think of cosmic kindnesses that have spared me such terrors, and I wonder, how much could I have taken before I broke? Before my eyes turned pale and dead? And once I broke, what would be left of me and would I ever be able to pick up the pieces?

*

My fascination with World War I doesn't end with the Treaty of Versailles. The barrage may have ceased, but the war's tides echoed in the Jazz Age's heightened rhythms. In the Lost Generation's disillusionment. In the surrealist's fragmented reality.

Perhaps the most unique post-war movement was Dada. Self-proclaimed as "anti-art," the Dadaists had survived the trenches but had lost their Gods. Like Vonnegut, they possessed no tools to make sense of a massacre, yet they couldn't remain silent. Instead, they turned a new mirror upon the world, a reflection of absurdity, images of a society that no longer made sense.

*

The Nazis didn't take kindly to the legacy of Dada, and works of that period, along with the Expressionists and other modern schools, were confiscated. In 1937, these pieces were exhibited in a converted hall in the Institute of Archeology in Munich. The show, entitled *Entartete Kunst* (Degenerate Art), drew over two million patrons during its run. Coinciding with the exhibit,

Goebbels arranged another show, this one in Munich's palatial House of German Art. The *Grosse duetsche Kuntausstellung*, which featured classical, state-sanctioned art free from Jewish and Bolshevik influences, opened amid great fanfare and featured fawning visits from Hitler and other top party leaders. At the end of four months, it had drawn less than a third of the audience of the *Entarte Kunst* exhibit.

*

"What are the horrors of war, no one can imagine."

—Florence Nightingale

*

Dr. Jacob Mendez de Costa studied veterans of the American Civil War. His patients, having survived the battlefield, returned home with odd afflictions. Tachycardia. Anxiety. Tremors. Paralysis. Shortness of breath. He christened the syndrome "Soldier's Heart." Around the country, physicians were noting similar symptoms in other soldiers, men who'd been perfectly healthy at the front but who, when returned to the quiet of home, began to exhibit this mysterious unraveling.

Men who suffered complete breakdowns were discharged, but by 1863, the number of such men, many of whom wandered the cities and countryside, impelled the government to establish the first military hospital for the insane. The hospital closed with the war's end, and in its place, a system of soldiers' rest homes was set up around the country. Hooray for the compassion that can follow savagery. A decade after the war's end, some directors of these homes noted the need for services had bucked their expected trends and increased with each passing year.

*

"I have participated in two wars and know that war ends when it has rolled through cities and villages, everywhere sowing death and destruction. For such is the logic of war. If people do not display wisdom, they will clash like blind moles and then mutual annihilation will commence."

—Nikita Khrushchev

*

Imagine Billy Pilgrim's journey. He passes the dead. On the battlefield. In the POW's cattle car. The multitude of Dresden. Poor old Edgar Derby. His wife. Billy's path, like all paths, leads him past death after death until he reaches his own. So it goes.

A few years ago, I decided to donate my body to a local teaching hospital. My shell will be cut open. Doctors-to-be will practice their techniques, their scalpels wielded to peel back skin and muscle, my ribcage cracked and opened like a party gift. They will note the bones that have broken and healed. They will consider my worn ligaments, hold my still heart.

In the same hospital sits the ER where I've been stitched and X-rayed. Four floors up, the room where my son was born. The same rhythms that once consumed me—the commuters' flow, the bike-path joggers, the bells of the nearby high school where I've taught for the past three decades—will continue as I lay gutted beneath bright lights. I've heard some students become quite fond of their cadavers, the dead given pet names and treated with respect, and I'm pleased by the thought that after I am done with this world, it will not quite be done with me.

There's a ceremony every spring for the bodies that have been used in the previous year. Some are cremated and returned to their families. The rest are buried, another mass grave yet different from Dresden and a thousand other bone-filled pits. Kind words are offered, prayers. The students attend, and in the crowd, a few family members. There are tears, hugs, a release of balloons, all eyes lifted to the sky. In the ground, a small marker, an engraving of thanks. In time, the crowd disperses. The seasons will pass. The landscapers will snip away the encroaching grass. The snows will bury the marker and the thaw will offer it back to the sun. If I am in that grave, I will accept the gratitude of the marker's words. If I was given the opportunity to create a stone of my own, I might use the words of Billy Pilgrim to greet the passers-by—

In the Hamidan Massacres of the1890s, between 200,000 and 300,000 Armenians and Syrians were slaughtered by the Ottoman Empire. Some reports claim entrepreneurs later dug up the mass graves and sold the bones on the black market, with many of the bones making their way to Europe to be ground into animal feed. The stews of a generation were a single, trophic level removed from murder. Stomach acids broke down the marrow. The clouds of war gathered across the continent.

*

My son and I hurry-step across a gravel lot, our eyes squinted against a biting wind. Ahead, an old German barn. A sloped roof, a fieldstone foundation. The barn a reminder of what was, the rich farmland that's been piecemealed into houses and strip malls. We step inside. My eyes water, the warmth sudden and welcome. The first level's uneven concrete floor remains. Strategic beams rise like tree trunks. All else has been claimed by small booths, shelves filled with knickknacks and detritus cleaned and polished, as if they'd never aged.

We've been coming here for years—rainy Saturdays, lazy summer afternoons, after-school stops. My son has cycled through his fascinations—hand tools, toy guns, political campaign buttons. Today's focus: dated technology. Brownie cameras and rotary phones, wind-up phonographs and reel-to-reel tape players. He asks questions, and I do my best to answer. In his mind, the fitting together of what was and what is. Vonnegut paints a quick portrait of Billy's mother as she visits him after his postwar breakdown: "Like so many Americans, she was trying to construct a life that made sense from things she found in gift shops." Take this stance, add the twist of time, and here we are, walking with ghosts, the once-owners who held these items as new. Those souls aged or gone, but their minutia remains, a reminder of what lasts and what doesn't.

Consider poor Edgar Derby. The father figure among the ragged children, shot over a teapot plucked from the smoldering ruins. The teapot, we infer, reminds him of home—perhaps in actuality, perhaps merely in symbolism, its unlikely survival a whisper of hope amid the nightmare. He looks back—to home, to what he's lost and what he yearns to return to—and pays with his life.

My son crouches, a finger turning an 8mm projector's take-up reel. I'm anxious to move along, but I wait, my patience rewarded when I spot a radio tucked along a higher shelf. It's a boxy thing, the size of a stout book, heavy in my hands, a leather case and telescoping antennae. I toggle the red switch between AM and FM, and in me, a sense of reunion, for I had the same model as a child, my son and I now adrift in separate, enraptured worlds. When I was his age, I stayed up late and worked the dial. I hear again the pop songs it played, the soundtrack of a fading generation. On clear nights, I sifted through the AM static, honing in on watery signals. Some from cities I knew. Others that sent me to our atlas, and I'd sit in the near dark and imagine all those strangers living in distant cities.

There's a swell in my chest, the tug of holding what's been lost. I think of Edgar Derby, his hands filled with a teapot that had survived so much. I think of each booth as its own time machine. Here is the lure of what we've left, the call of the past. Poor Kurt Vonnegut. Poor Edgar Derby. Poor Lot's wife. Can any of us ever stop looking back?

*

As a child, Henry Molaison suffered a severe head injury in a bicycle accident. The seizures that started afterward grew more frequent and intense as the years went on. In 1953, at the age of twenty-seven, Molaison underwent an experimental surgery to remove part of his hippocampus. The procedure proved successful in easing his seizures, but there was an unexpected side effect. The wires that allowed Henry to make new memories had been unhooked. Labeled simply HM in medical journals, Molaison became the most studied patient in the history of brain science. He remembered World War II and the Great Depression. He remembered his pre-surgery family and friends, but he proved incapable of making any new, long-term memories. He reportedly handled this situation with the good humor of a man beyond frustration, a man who greeted his nurses with the same polite introductions day after day, year after year, decade after decade. He became, as the Tralfamadorias would say, a bug trapped in amber.

After his death in 2008, Henry's doctors cut his frozen brain into 2,401 slices each .07 mm thick. The slices, frozen and beautifully textured, looked like bugs in amber.

*

Billy Pilgrim's eyes have beheld death and cruelty on an unimaginable scale. He's numb, polite, apologetic. He shrinks into the background. He observes. He means no harm, possesses no great drive. He staggers through the Dresden streets, a man lost in time.

The war is almost over, hallelujah and amen. Dresden has been abandoned by its defenders, and the Russians have yet to arrive. Billy Pilgrim and his mates roam, unclaimed but not yet liberated. They commandeer a cart and horse. They collect spoils of war, the type of knickknacks that got poor Edgar Derby shot. An old couple stops them. They are doctors, the speakers of many languages. They take the horse's reins and scold the Americans. Billy climbs from the cart. The doctors point out the horse's mouth, bloody and full of sores, and for the first time in the war, Billy breaks down in tears.

When does Billy cry again? Not when his plane crashes. Not when his wife dies. Not when his daughter begins to find joy in dictating his life. Billy keeps his steady course through all of that. He cries in his examination room as he peers into his patients' eyes. He cries in the dark in the company of near-strangers.

Billy Pilgrim tumbles along, blissfully adrift in his own life, a ghost of gray smoke. Then he takes pause. He examines the mouth of a mistreated horse. He looks beneath the curved surface of a patient's cornea. He cries when he considers the mechanics of our witnessing—the mouths that can't speak, the eyes that record the deeds of men.

*

World War I gave us the term "shell shock." At first, physicians believed the proliferation of field artillery and the front's days-long bombardments produced concussions that damaged the physiology of the brain, but as the war dragged on, doctors and commanders learned the affliction's roots ran deeper. The wounds these men received originated not in flesh but through the senses. The things they'd seen. The terror they'd felt. Commonly noted symptoms included tremors, anxiety, hallucinations, and sleeplessness.

The United States, a latecomer to the slaughter, sent nearly two million men to fight in Europe. Casualties—116,516 dead, 204,000 wounded. During that time, 159,000 soldiers were pulled from the lines to be treated for psychiatric conditions. Of these, nearly 70,000 were permanently discharged.

*

In the first letter Kurt Vonnegut wrote to his family after being released as a prisoner of war, he related his treatment at the hands of the Germans. He described his guards as "sadistic and fanatical." The prisoners were denied clothing and medical treatment. They were treated as slave laborers, a direct violation of the Geneva Convention. Their daily rations consisted of black bread and watery soup. Vonnegut, with his limited knowledge of German, was the prisoners' representative. After two months of fruitless pleading with their captors for better supplies, he told the guards what he was going to do to them once the Russians came. The guards promptly beat him up.

Slaughterhouse-Five overflows with brutality, but for the most part, Vonnegut paints his captors in forgiving tones. They are too young, too old, too wounded, looking to either surrender to the Americans or just survive another day. They are, like their prisoners, humans cast into an inhuman mess. It took Vonnegut over twenty years to write about his war experiences. Time has a way of softening the memory, but Vonnegut's portrayal goes beyond a simple letting go. He deliberately gives us a compassionate picture of his enemies, a rarity among us human-types who've been done wrong.

Forgiveness. Perhaps our country's finest hour came not in the war but in its aftermath. We punished the leaders in open trials and did not, as Stalin advocated at the 1943 Tehran Conference, round up and murder 50,000 German officers. Instead of pouring salt over the leveled cities, we helped raise the vanquished from the ashes. Stalin didn't get to kill his 50,000 officers, but the Soviets took conciliation by subjugating the next two generations of Eastern Europe.

Nations can forgive, but their motives are political or ideological. Vonnegut forgave, but it's easier to excuse strangers, fellow soldiers who owed him no allegiance. The forgiveness between intimates is different, the sting of betrayal personal, a pain often carried in secret, a poison in our guts. They are the fuel for ugliness. The fights, the words we later regret. They also offer us the chance to show a deeper, less tidy brand of love.

I have been forgiven, many times over. I hope I've learned from my mistakes and that I have, in my way, expressed my thankfulness. I have forgiven. These acts have freed me, but they've never been easy. I have yet to renege a forgiveness, but in moments of difficulty, when the hurt has resurfaced and tugged at my thoughts, I've wanted to remind another of what I've done. What I'm owed. Thankfully, I've stepped back and swallowed my pain. What I haven't always felt in my heart, I have achieved by shutting my mouth.

There are limits to forgiveness, each of us with our own thresholds. Here is my agnostic's prayer—that I will live my life without being forced to carry a hurt stronger than my best self. Amen and amen.

*

"This book is to be neither an accusation nor a confession, and least of all an adventure, for death is not an adventure to those who stand face to face with it. It will try simply to tell of a generation of men who, even though they may have escaped its shells, were destroyed by the war."

—Erich Maria Remarque,
preface to *All Quiet on the Western Front*

*

ECHOES IN THE LONG FLIGHT OF STAIRS THIS TWO-STORY THROAT OF CONCRETE AND NO ONE SAYS A WORD AND UP YOU GO WAITING YOUR TURN AND THROUGH THE DOOR AN ASHY

LIGHT AND THE STAB OF SMOKE THICKER WITH EACH STEP AND YOU'VE BEEN HERE BEFORE BUT NO THAT WAS YOUR BIRTH BUT THERE'S NO WARMTH NOW NO RED GLOW YET YOU ARE BEING BORN AGAIN AND YOU SPILL FORTH INTO A MOONSCAPE OF BRICK AND TIMBER AND BENEATH THE RUBBLE A HAND HERE AND A FOOT THERE THEN MORE AND YOU COVER YOUR MOUTH BUT IT'S TOO LATE THE SMOKE ALREADY A CURRENT IN YOUR LUNGS AND BLOOD

*

Merriam-Webster defines pornography as "the depiction of erotic behaviors (as in pictures or writing) intended to cause sexual excitement." Censors link pornography with the vile and grotesque. The exploitive. The dehumanizing. Most of these conversations revolve around nakedness and genitalia and penetration. The book banners' moral antenna tweak at *Slaughterhouse-Five*'s mentioning of blowjobs or the private peepshows of unclothed humans. Not viewed as pornographic is the penetration of metal into flesh or the roasting of children.

Behind enemy lines, Roland Weary shows Billy Pilgrim a photograph of a woman attempting intercourse with a Shetland pony. Their German captors confiscate the picture, and no interpreter is needed to understand their smiles. "What a lucky pony," the German corporal says. "Don't you wish you were that pony?" We learn the photograph is a reprint of film's first pornographic image. In court, the photographer declared the photo a work of art, a retelling of Greek myths. Why else would his picture have columns and a fancy curtain and a potted palm? Later, we find Billy in a New York City smut shop, drawn not by exposed body parts but by the window display's dusty collection of Kilgore Trout novels. One of the shop owners calls Billy over and offers to let him see the "hot stuff." From behind the counter, he produces the postcard of the woman and the pony. Here is the lure of Tralfamadorian thought, this girl who has stayed pretty and young, both she and the horse forever preserved.

Early 1976, and I was fifteen. The Bicentennial looming. Gerald Ford. I read Vonnegut. I read *National Lampoon*. I listened to Jimi Hendrix, The Stones, Jethro Tull. I wanted to kiss a girl, but I had no idea who or how, and in my veins, the jagged flow of want and confusion. Then my first experience with pornography beyond a page torn from *Playboy*. A frigid day, a clear sky, the snow deep and ice on the sidewalks. I can't call the boy I walked with a friend. We played basketball at the park. We said "Hey" when we passed each other in the hallway. I'd accepted a vague invitation. In a deserted house, he produced an 8mm projector and drew the blinds. Dust in the projector's white beam. No sound save the sprockets' jerk and tug. It would take me years to appreciate the film's brutality, two tattooed men in leather masks, the woman bound. The things they used on her. The reel lasted less than ten minutes, and as it spun on the take up, I made an excuse and a hasty exit. At a nearby playground, I wiped snow from a swing and sat, swaying. The cold bit into my lungs, and my eyes watered in the glean of sun on snow.

There's love. There's sex. Both good things, but pornography is neither. Pornography is commerce, a postcard sold, a website opened, and as such, I've placed it on the list of industries I can't support. In my twenties, I went to a few strip clubs. In my forties, I clicked a few links, but I couldn't give myself over. I drift into the hidden scene, the crew behind the camera's eye, the dream's cold reality. I weave narratives, and my desire wilts when I see these women as daughters who were once loved or not loved enough. I see runaways, women who hated school because they didn't fit in. I see women who only want to wipe out their pasts and pains in broad, defiant strokes.

For the book-banners of previous generations, a word like "blowjob" provided an easy excuse. They viewed the surface, the literal's thin ice, but not the depth of what waited beneath. Pornography might be relegated to society's margins, but Vonnegut reminds us there are greater obscenities. Obscenities not hidden beneath the artifice of a staged and captured image. Obscenities real and bloody and draped in the banners created by the writers of history.

*

Genghis Khan said, "The greatest joy for a man is to defeat his enemies, to drive them before him, to take from them all they possess, to see those they love in tears, to ride their horses, and to hold their wives and daughters in his arms." To Khan, rape of the conquered was simply a facet of war, and outside many cities under his siege, women threw themselves from the fortress walls, preferring death to the waiting brutality. Today, geneticists believe 1 in 200 men, about 16 million, carry Khan's Y chromosome.

As Soviet troops crossed into Germany, they launched a front behind the front, a frenzy of condoned rape. Military historians estimate the number of sexual assaults at at least two million, with many enduring multiple rapes. In Berlin itself, at least 100,000 women were raped, and of these, 10,000 died, either from trauma or suicide. Residents of Berlin, many of them women, their men dead, their windows blow out by explosions, recalled the sounds of night, the crying, the screams. The silence that followed a single gunshot.

*

Spot is Billy Pilgrim's dog. Billy loves Spot, and Spot loves Billy.

I never owned a dog until a few years ago, and since, I've been humbled by the unanticipated joy our dog has brought into our lives. He is all love, all devotion. He follows us everywhere. With a knock at the door, he charges into the vestibule, barking, hackles raised. Five minutes later, he's camped upon the visitor's lap. Much about him is a mystery, his age, his lineage's contrasting notes. He walks with a limp. He's missing teeth. He came to us at a rough juncture, all of us fragile, the midst of a long, cold winter. At the shelter, my son sat on the floor, and the dog came to him, silent, a sniffing inspection before he climbed onto his lap. "I think he's chosen you," the shelter owner said.

I'm thankful surprise still finds me. Love—there can never be enough. The dog spent his first nights in his crate, not a bark, but in less than a month, he was sleeping with my son. The dog sees us through the hard times. He becomes part of us. All he wants is to be near.

When we take him to an open field, he gallops his jerky stride across the grass, but on neighborhood walks, he's a sniffer, a thorough marker. At first I was impatient with a walk's tenth leg lift, his nudgings around streetlamps and trees, but then I read an article on a dog's sense of smell. A dog's snout isn't only a thousand times more sensitive than mine, it's also a gift that allows him to "see" into the past. An envisioning of another dimension. The moment's emptiness filled with ghosts.

I exhale, a plume of steam, this cold night. He pulls his leash taut. His black nose twitches as it investigates a brittle leaf. Who's a smart little doggie?

*

"Man does not control his own fate. The women in his life do that for him."

—Groucho Marx

*

The Gospel of Kilgore Trout

And it came to pass in those times when the shadow of war spread across the kingdom that certain duties of the sword proved too trying for the souls of Godly men. And so the wisest of men begat a servant that was as much man as it was not, for it walked with the steps of man and beheld the world with the eyes of man. Yet the servant had not a conscience nor had it a soul that would be troubled by the thought of burning flesh and the slaughter of multitudes, both of his enemy and the children of his enemy and the parents of his enemy and his enemy's beasts of burden. And lo, the servant was untroubled by the devastation sown beneath the shadow of his flying wings, and with his weapons, he did smite the enemy and darken his lands. For this, he was christened The Gutless Wonder.

And the Gutless Wonder appeared as man and talked as man and walked as man, and at the times of the feast, he danced and made merry with the young maidens as of the other young men and none held against the Gutless Wonder his deeds of dropping jellied gasoline onto the skin of tribes unlike theirs. Yet lo, the Gutless Wonder found himself an outcast for he carried the mark of halitosis and here was a sin for which there was no forgiveness, and for this, he was shunned until the day the stench was cleaned from his mouth. And with the scent of mint, the young and old of his tribe adopted him as their son and thought never of the fire he reined upon the lands of their foes.

*

Imagine the violence in *Slaughterhouse-Five* as a firestorm. Dresden burns in the night, a column of flame, destruction on a scale unseen since God's handiwork at Sodom. But a firestorm doesn't exist in isolation—it's fed by its own lethal currents, and consider the violent tides in Billy's life. He is beaten by Roland Weary, threatened and eventually murdered by Paul Lazaro. Billy walks like a costumed child through the crumbling Reich, bodies everywhere, smoke on the horizon. He sees a man hanged for making love to a woman of the wrong race. He smells candles made from the fat of murdered Jews. Later, he is the lone survivor of a horrific plane crash, his wife dying in her rush to be at his bedside.

Picture Billy Pilgrim in the eye of the storm. The flames swirl, sometimes touching him, a singe upon his flesh, yet he remains unfazed. He will break down in laughter during a production of *Cinderella.* He will break down when he's returned to the post-war peace of Illium, NY. He will break down in mysterious tears in his dark examination room and as he watches a cripple sell magazines door-to-door. Yet when the flames burn their hottest, Billy Pilgrim barely notices.

He, like the rest of our kind, has seen this all before.

*

In the novel's initial chapter, Vonnegut tells of his postwar work at a Chicago newspaper. His first story—the death of a young veteran, a boy who survived the war only to return home to be crushed to death after getting his wedding ring caught in an elevator's iron gate. Back in the newsroom, a jaded writer convinces Vonnegut to call the widow and pose as a police officer. The woman reacts as Vonnegut expected. She cries and tells him of a baby who would now grow up fatherless. Vonnegut hangs up, and the reporter who put him up to it eats a candy bar as she asks Vonnegut if the sight of the squished man bothered him.

No, Vonnegut says. He's seen plenty of bodies.

There is a numbness of the physical, and I think of the summers I worked in factories or construction crews, the wielding of wrenches and shovels, the blisters that hardened into calluses. I think of the twenty-year window when I could run five, seven, ten miles without strain, and in the midst of it all, the moment where I'd become disassociated from my body, reduced to head and feet and a wispy cloud in between.

Then there's the numbness of the soul. The first broken heart, the first lost friend—these rattle us but the next time is easier. We possess a sad touchstone, a toughening of tender spots. Billy Pilgrim learned to walk past a corpse without a second glance. The first one no doubt rattled him—its stillness, its gore and fragility, its reminder of waiting fate—but in war, there are a surplus of corpses, and Billy Pilgrim fashions a unique vision rooted in a belief that time had cast him like a dandelion seed blown this way and that along the B-theory's continuum.

Yet unlike Kilgore Trout's Gutless Wonder, this numbness isn't complete, and even those with the most intricate blinders will stumble across a scene that will stab their callused hearts. The pain of consciousness—we all have our limits, the scenes that burn so deeply we can't look away. Here is where my heart softens for the junkie. For the alcoholic who drinks to forget. For the broken soldiers lost in the loop of time. Here are the men and women failed by numbness and blinders. They can't accept the Tralfamadorian invitation to look past the ugliness. They can't escape the horrors they've witnessed. They become bugs trapped in amber, captured in a moment they can't escape.

*

Stalin's purges killed over 10 million. His chief executioner was Vasili Blokhin, who murdered thousands with a single shot from his custom German pistol. Prior to the Nazi invasion of the Soviet Union, Blokhin was sent to the section of Poland annexed by the Soviets in 1939. There, he reportedly shot three hundred men a night for twenty-eight straight days in the Katyn Massacre. In his official photo, his chest gleams with medals.

In 1937, the Imperial Japanese Army invaded Nanking. Researchers estimate between 40,000 to 300,000 civilians were murdered. Japanese military newspapers trumpeted the competition between sub-lieutenants Toshiaki Mukai and Tsuyoshi Noda. Their contest—who could be the first to kill one hundred men with their sword. The victims, mainly prisoners and civilians, were beheaded or run through. Final score: Mukai—106; Noda—105.

*

"Blessed be the LORD, my rock, who trains my hands for war and my fingers for battle." —Psalm 144:1

*

Give me one word to relate the central subject of *Slaughterhouse-Five*, and I would say "death." Give me one word to describe the book's tone, and I would say "humorous." Thank goodness no one is limiting me to single-word responses.

In a 2006 interview, Vonnegut contended his characters' laughter was often a response to inescapable agony, a reaction little different than sobbing. Listen to Freud address the phenomena: "the ego (of a suffering person) refuses to be distressed by the provocations of reality, to let itself be compelled to suffer. It insists that it cannot be affected by the traumas of the external world; it shows, in fact, that such traumas are no more occasions for it to gain pleasure."

Consider *Slaughterhouse-Five*'s dark humor. The hobo who continually asserts, "This ain't so bad" until he falls dead. The British POW enclave, well-fed and relentlessly cheery amid a wasteland of dying Russians. Poor Edgar Derby shot over a teapot in the midst of a ruined city. Billy's ridiculous outfit, the too-small woman's coat and silver boots. He is a soldier dressed like an oversized Tinkerbell with the heart of a child, innocent, weaponless, threatened more by his fellow Americans than by the enemy. Billy's first nervous breakdown comes in the prison camp as he watches the Brit's adult-themed version of *Cinderella*. Billy laughs so hard and long that he must be dragged from the makeshift theater, tied to a bed, and injected with morphine. Unable to cry, Billy breaks down and laughs at his world. What else can he do?

*

According to *Merriam-Webster*, the first known use of "gallows humor" was 1901, which is amazing considering the long history of gallows. Also noted in the entry is the term's rhyming with "baby boomer."

James D. French was the only prisoner executed in the United States in 1966. Already serving a life sentence and unwilling to commit suicide, he murdered his cellmate in an effort to compel the state of Oklahoma to execute him. The state obliged and on August 10th, he was strapped into the electric chair. His last words before the switch was thrown were to the event's reporters: "How's this for a headline? 'French Fries!'"

*

Between one to six percent of the population walk through their days carrying a brain aneurysm. They are bombs with unlit fuses. A bout of prolonged laughter increases the pressure inside the skull, and this in turn places stress upon the aneurysm. *Tick-tock* go the bombs, and who knows when they'll go off. A hearty belly laugh puts pressure on the abdominal wall. This can trigger a hernia. In rare cases, a hernia can become strangulated, which, if left untreated, can cause death due to a lack of blood to the bowel. People with COPD or coronary heart disease can die from the stress laughter places upon their already taxed systems.

The Greek philosopher Chrysippus died of laughing after seeing a donkey eat figs. The Greek painter Zeuxis is said to have died laughing after completing his painting of Aphrodite, a portrait whose model was the old woman who'd commissioned it. In 1975, Englishman Alex Mitchell died after twenty-five minutes of continual laughing over an episode of the BBC comedy *The Goodies*. His widow sent the show's makers a thank-you note for making her husband's final minutes so happy.

*

While we were being bombed in Dresden, sitting in a cellar with our arms over our heads in case the ceiling fell, one soldier said as though he were a duchess in a mansion on a cold and rainy night, 'I wonder what the poor people are doing tonight.' Nobody laughed, but we were still glad he said it. At least we were still alive! He proved it.

*

In the mid-sixties, Kurt Vonnegut took a teaching position at the Writers' Workshop at the University of Iowa. For the first semester, he lived alone. His older sons at college. His daughter finishing high school. His wife, Jane, back home.

In an early letter, he confessed to Jane that he'd gone to the movies the night before to see *The Umbrellas of Cherbourg*. He wrote: "I took (the movie) very hard. To an unmoored, middle-aged man like myself, it was heartbreaking. That's all right. I like to have my heart broken."

Our hearts break. It's a tender organ, after all, a constant laborer beneath its ribbed dome. Heartbreak. Surely the word owes much of its origin to metaphor, the heart's romantic ties to emotion and love. No amount of grit can stave heartbreak's bloodless stab or lift its weight from our shoulders. The ache refuses to leave, and we can only wish it to fade or become familiar. We can't stop its cycle into our consciousness, the surfacing that triggers a sigh, a moment of pause. Our deepest love is reserved for a select few, and when these bonds are broken or strained, we question if we're strong enough for this life.

Then there's a gentler type of heartache. The kind that can be brought on by a movie seen by a man who misses his wife. A moment's sting and an aftertaste of sweetness. With the years, one's physical and metaphorical hearts toughen, wary of their labor and hurt. This is natural, our emotional lives following arcs just as real as our physical ones. Our culture laments the loss of youth, but this is a short-sighted view. My fifty-year-old heart doesn't beat as strong as its twenty-year-old counterpart, yet it possesses its own gifts. An appreciation of beauty in all its unexpected forms. A deeper reservoir of empathy. An understanding of its kinship with all hearts, beating and not.

In *Slaughterhouse-Five*, Billy Pilgrim's heartbreak cuts so deep it severs the ties of reality. He has walked through the valley of the shadow of death. He carries scars. He hurts in body and soul. We feel for him even though he mourns for us. The horrors we are capable of. The ease with which we lose our way.

Yet the book is so light. The humor, of course. Vonnegut's language, passages simple and lulling. The two-minute sections, a trail of crumbs, a path that loops back upon itself again and again. Here waits the other type of heartbreak, the kind that swirls up, an ambushing tide. The kind, like the private in Vonnegut's slaughterhouse, that reminds us we're alive.

*

Merriam-Webster dates 1944 as the first usage of the word "genocide." The term's coinage is attributed to Raphel Lemkin, who combined the Greek *genos* (tribe) with the Latin *cide* (to kill).

Hooray for language, with its ability to evolve! Hooray for our growing and living vocabulary!

*

My alarm goes off at 5:30. In truth, it's not yet 5:00, but it's easier to greet 5:30 than 4:45. I have my share of quirks. Another quirk—the clock itself. I bought it thirty-two years ago, a strip mall Radio Shack, a space that's been revamped into a new franchise at least once in each ensuing decade.

The radio's reception is poor. The volume only functions at certain levels—the whisper, the shout, and a thin, watery band in between. I should have replaced it years ago, but then I thought of all the mornings I'd woken to those red digits. The apartments I can barely remember. The house I've bought, and in which, God willing, I'll die. I will buy a new clock this summer, one absolutely futuristic in comparison. But these are my last few months as a public high school teacher, and I want to finish my run with the clock that has coaxed me into consciousness all these years.

I prefer to wake to voices. I like to lie still and let the tide of understanding rise in me. I rarely hit snooze. The morning hour is quiet, my brain unbothered, and with the warmth of coffee in my throat, I write. Engaged. Clear-headed. Happy.

The clock's pace has quickened this past year. A fault of circuits, new minutes gained every few days. Time in our bedroom has become an estimate, a best guess, a joke on me, on all of us, for hasn't time been speeding up all along, the years compressing, growing shorter? My body slows, but the momentum pushes me along, faster and faster.

*

"Clocks slay time . . . time is dead as long as it is being clicked off by little wheels; only when the clock stops does time come to life."   —William Faulkner

*

"Tomorrow, and tomorrow, and tomorrow,
  Creeps in this petty pace from day to day."

—William Shakespeare

*

In 1867, Alfred Nobel patented his most famous invention. Using the Greek *dýnamus* (power), he gave the world dynamite. He used his fortune to establish the Nobel Prize, an annual honoring of leading innovators in fields such as physics, chemistry, medicine, and literature. Many believe Nobel's decision to include a prize for peace was influenced by his long-time correspondence with Countess Bertha von Sutter, a prominent figure in the European pacifist movement and the first recipient of the Nobel Peace Prize. In 1891, he told the Countess: "Perhaps my factories will put an end to war sooner than your congresses: on the day that two army corps can mutually annihilate each other in a second, all civilized nations will surely recoil with horror and disband their troops."

Neither Nobel nor the Countess lived to see the outbreak of WWI.

*

Kilgore Trout, the reclusive science fiction author, says this to Billy Pilgrim: "Writing is like opening the window and making love to the world."

In interviews, I have cited my thankfulness for having found my creative niche in this world of distractions. I'm not one of those who knew they wanted to write from an early age, the child who filled diaries, the editor of the high school paper. When I reached my late twenties, I found myself somewhat settled—married, content with my career—yet I itched with the desire to create. I'd toyed with other media—woodwork, 8mm films. Then I wrote a story, and since, hardly a day has passed where I haven't put pen to paper.

Vonnegut's voice—humane, sardonic, honest—threads the roots of what calls me. I can't—nor want to—write like him, but I can't deny his presence, and for that, I'm a better artist. Kilgore Trout pictured an open window. I'll picture a cave, a journey inward and darkness all around. My questions form the dimmest of lights. I strain to see. I can't say if what awaits me is truth, but no matter. The struggle to understand is truth enough.

I've done well in the small world of literary publishing, yet I stumble when I think of calling myself a writer. A writer—it sounds too final, like I've reached a destination. But there is no destination; there's only practice, a continual reach. A desire to share a clear thought. A sentence's simple perfection. If I'm lucky, I will write until the period of my death. Until then, I will keep practicing, losing myself in the pages on my desk. I will embrace this chance to not mess up a gift of doing something honest and true. I will keep stumbling through the cave. I will keep opening my window and making love to the world.

*

Where do I get my ideas from? You might as well have asked that of Beethoven. He was goofing around in Germany like everybody else, and all of a sudden this stuff came gushing out of him. It was music. I was goofing around like everybody else in Indiana, and all of a sudden stuff came gushing out. It was disgust with civilization.

*

Count backward a hundred years and witness our kind's inventiveness. We've been to the moon. We've cured diseases. A wireless connection circles the globe, a sharing of images and ideas. No strides have been greater than our ever-more efficient ways of killing our fellow man, a tally much padded by the invention that made Alfred Nobel a rich man. A hundred years, and at the start of WWI, airplanes weren't armed, and the rival pilots saluted each other as they passed. They called themselves knights of the air, a chivalry fated to whither in the nightmare. Fast forward to the next Great War. The squadrons that blackened the skies over London, Hamburg, Tokyo, and Dresden. Below, ruined cities, fires that would rage until there was nothing left to consume. The bodies of civilians—the frontline soldiers of total war.

As Americans, we've allowed ourselves to become numbed by the cognitive dissonance of wartime bombing. We see the victims when they look like us—Oklahoma City, New York, Boston—but our vision turns murky when we consider cities outside our borders. We ignore the fact that intelligent weapons aren't perfect, and that our nation's toll of innocents killed far surpasses that of every terrorist attack on US soil. We wouldn't stand for our troops marching into Hiroshima and running their bayonets through seventy thousand civilians. We would cry out against the gallows erected on every street corner of Cologne, the hangmen busy day and night, the bodies stacked like wood. Death is still death, be it with a bullet to the back of the head or from a plane flying high above the clouds. Yet the nose-camera videos filmed from afar bring us comfort. Few among us would care to gaze into a dying man's eyes, but a distant explosion, a plume of smoke, a collapsed building—these carry the gift of anonymity, and the comfort allows us the luxury of ignoring the moment's human toll.

It can be argued that Paul Lazaro is *Slaughterhouse-Five*'s villain. Mean, hateful, spurred by revenge and malice, Lazaro eventually keeps his oft-repeated promise to murder Billy Pilgrim. Yet in the war's venue of indiscriminate death, Lazaro possesses his own, twisted morality. He takes no joy in the carnage of Dresden. He doesn't hurt anyone who, in his skewed view of justice, didn't have it coming. He kills a dog that bit him, but he doesn't seek to kill all dogs. He fells Billy Pilgrim with a single shot, not with a bomb that rips through the auditorium. No such allowances were given by the Lancasters and B-17's of WWII. Our weaponry evolved—incendiaries, phosphorous, napalm. We could kill thousands and never be bothered by looking into another pair of eyes.

Hiroshima and Nagasaki were the war's cherry toppings. A single device, a flash hotter than the sun. New ways to die, carbon shadows cast upon the pavement, and further out, a sickness as patient as it was deadly—days, weeks, months. The war was won. There were parades and tears. Prosperity followed—we'd earned the good times through our victory over darkness, and here might be the greatest miracle of the past seventy years—no country has used a nuclear device since. The day will come when this threshold will be crossed again, and when it does, we will hold our breath, knowing we have lost our balance and a stumble could kill us all. Until then, let's give a nod to Alfred Nobel. Perhaps we've finally found a weapon too terrible to use, his belief correct, his timing just a little off.

*

"I want to say, and this is very important: at the end we lucked out. It was luck that prevented nuclear war. We came that close to nuclear war at the end. Rational individuals: Kennedy was rational; Khrushchev was rational. Castro was rational. Rational individuals came that close to total destruction of their societies. And that danger exists today."
—Robert McNamara

*

"I do not know what weapons World War III will be fought with, but World War IV will be fought with sticks and stones." —Albert Einstein

*

Thirty-three years in public education, and I've seen my share of initiatives and reforms. Waves have passed. Curriculum has changed, changed back, changed again. We've championed Maslow, Danielson, Thompson, and back to Danielson. For the past decade we've jumped through the hoops of No Child Left Behind. We've been asked to achieve ever-higher test scores while also addressing a growing array of social ills—drugs, mental health, racism, violence, suicide, bullying, the disintegration of the traditional family. My career started with the Reagan administration's *Nation at Risk* report, and it will end with the first, stumbling years of The Common Core. I'm leaving soon, my time done, and without me, the pendulum will continue to swing. I think of Tennyson and a poem my father once read to me. "Ours is not to reason why . . ."

The Common Core brings a shift in focus. A little less of this, a little more of that, a tweaking of shiny technology. Old standards gussied up for a new decade. One of the more significant changes comes in literature. High school reading lists will be at least 75% nonfiction, the remaining quarter a dogfight between novels and stories, plays and poetry. Here's what I remember about high school English—Gatsby's parties, Pamplona's bulls, Harrison Bergeron's gravity-defying dance, a red wheelbarrow left in the rain. I remember because we took the time to talk about them. To imagine them. To feel them. Now I understand why so much depends upon a red wheelbarrow glazed with rain. At seventeen, I didn't.

All is not hopeless. The heritage of nonfiction is rich, its voices, its truths. This is my fear—the interests behind the Core don't desire a country of literature lovers but of proficient manual readers and report writers. Education, like our prison system and congressmen's votes, has become another product to sell, and the results of sharing and discussion and contemplation don't translate well to a multiple-choice response.

I enjoy writing essays, the quest for clarity, the puzzle of divining form in the formless. A well-written piece of nonfiction will stay with me longer than a story, the sharing of experience with those both like and unlike me, all of us inhabitants of this rock. But an educational system driven by the collection and interpretation of data can only lead to the call for more data. The scores pile up, and those in charge of shaping curriculum chase their magic numbers, losing sight of the value of imagination and freewheeling thought. Poetry, fiction, and drama offer the pleasure of immersion, that rare opportunity to dive beneath the facts and ponder a heart laid bare.

This is the setting my son will come up through. In three years, he'll enter high school, and I doubt there's enough time for the pendulum to swing back. I will do my best to share with him what he's missing. I will make sure he reads about a wheelbarrow left in the rain.

*

I believe reading and writing are the most nourishing forms of meditation anyone has so far found. By reading the writings of the most interesting minds in history, we meditate with our own minds and theirs as well. This to me is a miracle.

*

As I held that radio from my youth in the antique barn, what I felt wasn't so much reunion as a type of surfacing, the rising of the past into the present. For Billy Pilgrim, the years melt, and the linked heads of a barbershop quartet are supplanted by memories of his German captors. This layering exists throughout the book. An underlying network of times and events. A structure reminiscent of the child's board game of *Chutes and Ladders*. Billy Pilgrim, after pulling a blanket over his head or wandering through a door, finds himself cast across time, the blanket pulled down or the threshold crossed into a new reality.

Billy Pilgrim was twenty-two when he emerged from the slaughterhouse and into the moonscape of Dresden. At twenty-two, I was thoughtlessly strong. I lifted weights, churned out push-ups and pull-ups until I lost count. I jogged off hangovers. I witnessed my share of sunrises. With luck, I could have survived a war. I could have learned to walk past fallen soldiers without a second glance. At fifty-five, I understand I would never have been strong enough to shake off the experience of stacking the bodies of women and children and watching them burn.

We all have nightmares, but perhaps what separates scars that heal from those that don't depends upon whether we've been forced to live a nightmare with eyes opened wide. Kurt Vonnegut was a child plucked from the warm center of the American Midwest and deposited in faraway Dresden. He witnessed the darkness of our kind, and here waits the strange physics of memory, the images that sink then rise on their own volition, a fickle buoyancy over which one has scant control. Vonnegut had to write about Dresden, and I've got to believe even when he wasn't writing about Dresden, he was still writing about Dresden. What other choice did he have? How could one ever stop the continual surfacing of such memories?

*

The Dresden atrocity, tremendously expensive and meticulously planned, was so meaningless finally that only one person on the entire planet got any benefit from it. I am that person. I wrote this book, which earned a lot of money for me and made my reputation, such as it is. One way or another, I got two or three dollars for every person killed. Some business I'm in.

*

If I could draw, I'd be a visual artist. The medium's immediacy appeals to me, its universal communication. I'm especially captivated by twentieth century collagists and assemblers, the ones who reimagined the detritus of consumerism into art—Rochenberg, Hoch, Rodchenko, Cornell. My eyes wander over their pieces, the disparate harmonies, the logic of dreams. The layers and blurred boundaries. In its own fractured way, collage is a truer take on life than a single scene, for here waits the flotsam and random snippets we struggle to knit into a whole.

Vonnegut tried for twenty years to write his Dresden novel. In the first chapter, he describes his early attempts to shape his story. He claimed his best outline, or at least the prettiest, was drawn on the back of piece of old wallpaper. He used his daughter's crayons, his characters horizontal lines, each a different color. The lines tangled here, drifted there. They stopped with a character's death. A dark vertical band marked the bombing of Dresden, and the lines that survived passed through to the other side.

But Vonnegut couldn't make his story march up and down Freytag's Pyramid. Instead, he offers us a shredded narrative, snapshots and tangents, a main character so scarred he's been expelled from the certainty that one second will follow another. Here's what took Vonnegut twenty years to realize—the rationality of a linear narrative would be an injustice when telling a story of madness.

After dinner. My son with his homework, the dishes done. I find myself online, sifting through images of Dresden, before and after. Hollowed buildings, a moonscape of rubble. Other photos taken without the luxury of distance. Roasted bodies. The children who believed they lived in a safe city. The human pyramids before the torch. I can see these images, but I'll never feel the heat rising from the stones. Never gag on the stench of days-old death.

I log out. Son and dog by my side, I set out for an evening walk. An early snow blankets the lawns, the stars above, and a hundred lit windows shine out to us. Steam rises from our mouths, this living mist, three soft machines together in the cold. I glance toward the windows, dioramas of normalness. I try to imagine them as burnt husks, but I can't. I just can't.

*

Another passage from *Slaughterhouse-Five*'s first chapter—Vonnegut offering the following apology when he finally handed his publisher his Dresden manuscript:

"It is so short and jumbled and jangled, Sam, because there is nothing intelligent to say about a massacre. Everybody is supposed to be dead, to never say anything or want anything ever again. Everything is supposed to be very quiet after a massacre, and it always is, except for the birds.

"And what do the birds say? All there is to say about a massacre, things like '*Poo-tee-weet?*'"

*

> The larks, still bravely singing, fly
> Scarce heard amid the guns below.
> We are the Dead.
>   —John McCrea, "In Flanders Fields"

*

Wilfred Owen was one of the First World War's most renowned poets. He fought with the Manchester Regiment during the Battle of the Somme. Wounded in both spirit and body, he was sent home to convalesce at Craiglockhart War Hospital, a facility that specialized in treating shellshock. He wrote of himself and his fellow patients: "There are the men whose minds the Dead have ravished / Memory fingers in their hair of murders / Multitudinous murders they once witnessed."

Late in the summer of 1918, Owen returned to the front lines, and for his bravery in battle, he was awarded the Military Cross. He was killed in action during the war's final week. According to the Wilfred Owen Association, Owen's mother received the telegraph informing her of her son's death on Armistice Day as the church bells rang in celebration.

*

On October 18, 1916, after a twenty-minute court martial, British Private Harry Farr was executed by firing squad. His crime—refusing to go over the top in another attack during the summer of the Somme. According to military records, Farr had fought for nearly two years with little time away from the front. No previous charges had been filed against him.

Farr was one of 306 members of the British Expeditionary Force executed for desertion or cowardice. Ninety years after his execution, Farr and the others were pardoned by the British government. Hooray for justice, albeit late and of little consequence for those gunned down to reinforce to the men in the trenches that there was as much to fear behind them as there was on the other side of No-Man's Land.

The 2012 edition of the US military's *Manual for Court Martial* still contains a provision for the death penalty for wartime desertion. According to a 2007 NBC report, Army stateside desertions were up 80% since the 2003 Iraq invasion.

*

As Billy Pilgrim recovers from his second nervous breakdown, he reads a book in a doctor's waiting room. *The Execution of Private Slovick* by William Bradford Huie details the account of Eddie Slovick, the lone US serviceman executed for desertion during World War II. First declared 4F due to his criminal record, Slovick was later drafted as the need for soldiers grew. Slovick preferred the stockade, a life that made more sense to him than the front lines. He offered to work in supply areas or mess halls, but he wasn't going to carry a gun. Of the forty-nine soldiers condemned to death for desertion during WWII, Slovick's was the only sentence carried out.

*

"They're not shooting me for deserting the United States Army, thousands of guys have done that. They just need to make an example out of somebody, and I'm it because I'm an ex-con. I used to steal things when I was a kid, and that's what they're shooting me for. They're shooting me for the bread and chewing gum I stole when I was twelve years old." —Eddie Slovick

*

Some basic divisions in the study of time:
<u>Physical Time</u>—the time of clocks and stopwatches and calendars. It's public time, agreed to by a civilized society, its roots made uniform by the railroad tycoons of the nineteenth century.

Biological Time—the body's sense of time, circadian rhythms and such. A time in flux, influenced by sunlight and darkness, the changing seasons, the mysterious turnings of our internal gears.

Psychological time—one's unique awareness of physical time. Psychological time passes quickly when we're enjoying the moment; not so much when we're squirming beneath the dentist's drill. The seconds themselves do not change. Only our attention to them.

Psychological time grows faster as one ages. Think of the summer vacations of youth—the weeks that stretched forever. Or the anticipation of the days leading up to Christmas. Adults of a certain age are often ambushed by their own birthdays, the calendar's pages turned, another year gone.

*

Joseph Heller was a friend and contemporary of Vonnegut. Both were WWII veterans, writers who used their art to expose war's toll on the human psyche. Heller's *Catch-22* is a classic of war literature, a tale of the military's absurd bureaucracy.

One of the novel's most interesting characters is Dunbar. Like the novel's protagonist Yossarian, Dunbar is one of the few men who seem to grasp the fact there's an actual war being fought. Like Yossarian, he doesn't want to die. How does he do this? He withdraws. He embraces boredom. He says little. He lies silent on his cot. Through inaction, he attempts to make time pass slowly, believing that by expanding the moment, he may actually live longer.

Perhaps Dunbar is on to something. Turn this slothful contention inside out and picture the lowly fly. Scientists have determined a housefly can react four times faster than us humans. The smaller an animal and the quicker its metabolic rate, the slower time passes. Some researchers believe this also extends to our species, with the littlest among us experiencing an expanded sense of the passing hours, and in my thoughts, a grudging compassion for the backseat refrain:

Are we there yet?

Are we there yet?

Are we there yet?

Dunbar, motionless, mute, his psychological clock ticking slower and slower, contemplated his own death, and in his thoughts, a similar refrain:

I'm not there yet.

I'm not there yet.

I'm not there yet.

*

Roland Weary staggers alongside Billy behind enemy lines, another child in the children's crusade. But not all children are kind. Weary lectures Billy on the science of torture. Thumbscrews. The Iron Maiden. Blood gutters. Weary waves his trench knife in Billy's face. The knife is special—a gift from his father, a triangular blade, a maker of wounds not meant to close. Billy is tempted to share that he knows a thing or two about gore. His childhood bedroom, the crucifix he fell asleep beneath every night. A pitiful Jesus, damaged and frail, crafted with disturbing anatomically correctness, His side pierced by a spear tip, a wound that wouldn't close.

Weary is the heartbeat, the breathing now, of the animal that closed the Iron Maiden. That set fire to a thousand cities. That nailed men to the cross. Weary has been with us forever, and he has the hardware to prove it.

Irony: Weary's boots are confiscated by a young boy at his capture. They switch shoes, but the boy's clogs tear at Weary's feet. He staggers on their forced march across the countryside, cursing and blaming Billy. He develops gangrene. Weary, the man fascinated by torture, dies walking in another man's shoes.

A sad truth: All Billy has to do is look around to find a thousand others anxious to take Weary's place.

*

One can literally walk in another's shoes, but is it possible to walk in them while the other person is still wearing them? Of course not . . . unless one enters the murky realm of quantum entanglement. Researchers are now able to isolate two atoms on opposite ends of a lab and coax them to share a proton. Despite their distance, they exist in tandem, their singular realities twinned, the stimulation of one simultaneously experienced by the other.

That's fine for atoms, but what about us human types? While the science of people-sized quantum entanglement may be beyond us now, there are some who can tell us what the future may hold. Sufferers of mira-touch synesthesia experience the sensations and emotions of those around them. Brain scans have revealed these neurological curiosities exhibit heightened responses in the brain centers associated with empathy. We've all cried at movies, felt the drop in our stomachs watching a 3-D film of a hurtling roller coaster. Now picture experiencing such sensations continually. Imagine feeling the pain of a stranger's stubbed toe. Imagine being a bar's only sober patron yet your head still spins. Those with the condition often complain of gagging when forced to watch others eat.

It's no surprise some with mira-touch synesthesia have become recluses. They draw the curtains, turn off the TV. I can't blame them. Who would want to take on the suffering of the entire human race?

*

One of history's most notorious torture devices was the Sicilian bull. Designed by Perillos of Athens for Phalaris, the ruler of Akragus, Sicily, the bull was a hollow, bronze sculpture with a single door. The victim was stuffed inside, and beneath, a fire lit. The metal heated, and the condemned slowly roasted to death. The bull's head contained a system of tubes that turned the prisoner's screams into a sound resembling a bull's bellowing. Accounts stated when the bull cooled and the door opened, the victim's bones shone like jewels.

Phalaris, a noted tyrant with an alleged taste for cannibalism, was overthrown in 540 BC. His captors roasted him in his prized bronze bull.

*

Slaughterhouse-Five is broken into over a hundred sections. Some are just a paragraph or brief conversation. Most no longer than a page or two. Vonnegut claimed this terse construction was rooted in his experience as a newspaper reporter. That medium dictated succinctness, and Vonnegut, the good soldier he was, spent much of his life marching to the rhythm. Think of each section as a frame, an outline for a moment observed, each a picture. Of pain. Of truth. Of humor. Think of *Slaughterhouse-Five* as a gallery where these portraits choke the walls. The frames hang this way and that. A hundred different perspectives that form a single mosaic.

Vonnegut sometimes discussed his struggles with depression. The darkness that came and went. His retreats into himself. The pull of thoughts, the things he'd seen. He claimed he, like many writers, carried within him "twenty acres of Sahara Desert." I see him in that desert, and I feel for his loneliness, his distance. I feel for the footprints he left and the emptiness all around.

As a teen, I viewed Billy Pilgrim's story as Vonnegut's. Time travel, aliens—they were fluff, the story's core waiting in Vonnegut/Pilgrim's war experiences. I started writing in my late twenties, and as I grew to appreciate the tricks of the craft, my perspective changed. Billy Pilgrim was a tool of expression, a marionette dancing on pulled strings.

I'm now as old as Billy Pilgrim at his death, and I must reconsider my stance. Billy Pilgrim is neither a puppet nor a doppelganger. Billy Pilgrim is a frame. He is the border Vonnegut constructed around his wounded soul. Within waited the picture he needed to show the world.

*

As an optometrist, Billy Pilgrim thrived. He drove a Cadillac, opened branch offices, lived in a fine house. His success was due in large part to a local factory that required all of its 68,000 employees to own a pair of safety glasses. Billy tested their vision and ground their lenses—but he also knew the optometrists' secret—that "frames are where the money is."

*

Groundhog Day starring Bill Murray and Andie McDowell was released in 1993. The story's premise—while covering the February 2nd festivities in Punxsutawney, PA, Murray's snarky and self-centered weatherman, Phil Connors, becomes trapped in a twenty-four-hour time loop. Each morning Sonny and Cher sing "I Got You, Babe" on his clock radio. Each morning at the bed and breakfast he endures the same meaningless conversations. Murray struggles to break free, but when he realizes his impotence, he grows increasingly despondent. Even suicide is beyond him. In time, he accepts his fate, and with it comes a change of heart. He betters himself. He becomes kind. He finds love, and with a kiss, the cycle is broken.

Upon its release, *Groundhog Day* was generally well received, and it ranked thirteenth among 1993's highest-grossing films. Yet like Murray's weatherman, the movie itself has defied the general trajectory of time, and instead of fading, its popularity has swelled. Much of this is thanks to cable TV, the film cycling through every winter, and on February 2nd, one can count on at least one station dedicating its programming to a *Groundhog Day* Marathon. Like *It's a Wonderful Life*, *Groundhog Day* has evolved to talk to us in a manner deeper than its original intent. The title itself has worked its way into our language, a reference for the drudgeries we can't escape. In 2007, *Groundhog Day* was noted as military slang for any new day of a soldier's tour of duty in Iraq.

*

The Gospel of Kilgore Trout

And the visitor traveled many miles, and lo, he came through the desert and into the valley of man. The valley's wise men shared their sacred text and the secrets of their gospel, yet the visitor remained without peace, not understanding the beauty of the word and the cruelty that lived in the valley and in the hearts of those who professeth to live by the gospel.

The visitor, after much thought, pointed to the sacred text and proclaimed, "Here is the fault of your ways, for your savior is the son of God."

The wise men shrunketh in horror, asking, "How can that be? How else would man know he was so loved by his Lord, God?"

The visitor paused, then spoketh: "Is it not wrong to kill the Son of God?"

The wise men nodded. "Yes," they cried, "this is the truth."

And the visitor spoketh again. "But the nameless others? The ones hung upon a thousand different crosses? What of them?"

The wise men looked one upon the other, their long beards scratched, their eyes vexed. And the visitor, seeing their confusion, spoketh: "Your savior should preacheth the same sermons and words, but be one of the uncounted and unwashed. Then, on the cross, your God should take him as his child."

And lo, a chorus rose from the wise men. "Why?" they asked. "Why?"

And the visitor spoketh: "For here would be his message, that I am always among you, and there is no greater sin than harming a bum who has no connections."

*

Billy Pilgrim, alone in the post-celebratory quiet following his daughter's wedding, plops in front of the television with a bottle of flat champagne. Having visited this moment many times before, he knows he has a few hours until the Tralfamadorian spaceship will come for him, so he watches a movie about American bombers in WWII and their brave crews. Only Billy, having become unstuck in time again, views the film in reverse. Wounded planes take off backward. Over France, German fighters pull back, sucking bullets and shell fragments from the planes and their crews. The fighters also repair the downed bombers and help raise them back to their squadrons. The bombers return to a German city, open their bomb bay doors, and lift their explosives, putting out a hundred fires along the way. When the squadron returns safe and sound to the base, their bombs are unloaded and shipped back to the United States, where they are dismantled and their harmful minerals buried back into the earth. The bomber crews turn in their uniforms and become normal high school students again. Billy, exhausted and tipsy, then adds his own chapter to the backwards movie, and Hitler turns into a baby, and everyone else turns into a baby, and all mankind dwindles back to make two perfect people named Adam and Eve.

Here is one of the book's sweetest fantasies—the notion that even the most horrible deeds can be redressed. That life can be rescued from death. That the monsters of this world were once innocents. In one of his last interviews, Vonnegut joked that the looming end of life made him want to return to his Indiana home. Not so much the place as to the time of safety and purity. A beautiful idea, and he chuckled, acknowledging he, unlike Billy Pilgrim, could never go back to being a nine-year-old.

Loss of innocence. Going home. Writers have made entire careers with these themes. I also feel the pull of those times, but my focus is muddled. For me, there exists no vivid moment, no day so perfect that I'd sacrifice now for then. Years from today, I will watch the backward movie of my life. The film will straighten my spine. It will shrink my tumors and repair my failing organs. It will bring back those I've lost. I will be taken to a day like today. A day where I'm not sick, where I'm not a burden. A day where I can wake up beneath the same roof with those I love. Let the film stop here—today—and let me live these hours with an awareness that underlies every action I take and every word from my mouth.

*

I'm on the road early. A cool October Saturday. An hour's ride and as I turn into the campus I attended thirty-five years before, I find myself anxious. The intramural fields, long and open between far-flung lecture halls, are already marked with orange cones. Above, dozens of Frisbees, warm-up throws, spots of white against the slate clouds. A throw lifts on a gust, the wind always tricky on this open swath, and a man less than half my age runs it down, a burst of speed, the catch made to look easy. In the parking lot, I spot the other SUVs and a clump of father types, and I park beside them.

I discovered Ultimate Frisbee in college. It took a few semesters to become proficient with an array of throws, and it took a little longer to understand my place on a field that often felt wide and confusing. After college I banded together with old teammates and we formed a club team that rolled to weekend tournaments anywhere within a tank of gas. I was a decent thrower. I caught the passes tossed my way but lacked the athleticism to make the plays that could turn a game's tide. I was a hustler, a point on our zone defense, a runner of road races on weekends unclaimed by tournaments, but I could be beat in a field-long sprint. By the time I reached my mid-thirties, the proverbial lost step had lengthened into two, and I bid my goodbye to one of the few sports I actually loved.

I climb from my car. A small shout goes up, and with the welcome, my anxiety fades. There are handshakes and hugs. We make jokes about ambulances and CPR and broken hips. Their faces are the same in the most important of ways, just a blurring around the edges, another shade of gray on this overcast morning.

I lace up my cleats and take a warm-up jog. I've kept in shape, but not the kind of condition the sport requires. My cleats bite into the earth, and yes, I remember this feeling. When the time comes, I line up. The field stretches, a longer view than what I'd remembered. Ten have showed from our old team, and on the other side, at least twenty college kids. Another game begins on an adjoining field. There are physical worries—the very real possibility of injury, my old man's body and this young man's game. And there are worries beyond muscle and bone—the concern that my play will betray what was, both to me and my teammates. Some memories are better left undisturbed.

The game begins, and thankfully, the college players are kind, their team broken into two squads. Our team jumps out to a surprising lead, helped by the wind and the use of the zone defense we ran so long ago. I'm lucky to snag a couple goals and throw for a few more. I also drop an easy pass, and more than once, I overthrow a teammate, remembering the young men who once ran as fast as I did. By the second half my hamstrings tighten. I stumble, a tweak in my ankle that I'll carry for the next two months. We suffer our first injuries—teammates helped to the sidelines, a swollen ankle, a twisted knee, and we're left with a single sub. A few points drag on, the wind kicking up, my stride shortening until I feel as if I'm barely moving. We hold on to win the first game, and with a pair of players borrowed from other teams, we manage to win a second.

Afterward, we gather at a local bar. I'm sore, and easing onto a stool proves to be a wincing affair. We have a beer and eat. We tease each other—how we've aged, the things we're no longer capable of. We tell stories. We ask questions, filling in the gaps of years, the children we've never met, the marriages that have lasted and faded. In my thoughts, this book and the themes of revisiting and reliving—the latter impossible, the former precarious—and I feel fortunate that today turned out so well. We leave generous tips, a token of thanks. A final gathering in the parking lot, talk of a tournament next spring, but I know this will be my last game.

The ride home passes quickly. I'm tired yet buoyed by the day's gifts, the rare opportunity to go back, to run with friends, to play a game that means nothing beyond a field's boundaries. I've been allowed a rare passage through time, my body changed, my perspective tinted by the years.

*

"How did it get so late so soon? It's night before it's afternoon. December is here before it's June. My goodness how the time has flewn. How did it get so late so soon?"

—Dr. Seuss

*

In WWII, the US Army made a concerted effort to ease psychological casualties. Using the day's most modern tests, draftees were screened in order to identify those who might crack beneath the pressure of battle. Based on these results, over five million men were rejected for military service. Still, some 500,000 US soldiers were lost due to what the Army termed "combat neurosis," or, as the war dragged on, "combat exhaustion."

In October of 1944, General Dwight Eisenhower distributed a report from the US Surgeon General addressing the psychological impact of war. The report stated: "[T]he danger of being killed or maimed imposes a strain so great that it causes men to break down. One look at the shrunken, apathetic faces of psychiatric patients . . .

sobbing, trembling, referring shudderingly to 'them shells' and to buddies mutilated or dead, is enough to convince most observers of this fact."

American commanders, using this report and their own experiences, estimated the average soldier could last about two hundred days in combat before suffering substantial psychological injury.

As of early 2013, almost 37,000 American troops had been deployed to Iraq and/or Afghanistan more than five times. Almost 400,000 service members had done three or more tours.

*

Billy Pilgrim is lost in the narrative of his own life. The situation is unique, his path haywire, yet the concept of individual-as-traveler in a cyclical loop is addressed in a number of the world's major religions. The Hindus give us Moksha, the liberation of a soul from the cycle of birth and death. Moksha brings not a Christian notion of heaven but a merging of an individual soul (*atman*) into the soul of the Supreme Being (*paramatman*).

The Buddhists offer the concept of Nirvana. Nirvana means "to extinguish." It is seen not as an end, nor simply as a deliverance from suffering and pain, but as a passing from one existence to another. The Buddha taught that a fire becomes visible when it meets a fuel—and returns to the invisible when it's released from the fuel. To extinguish is to be freed from time itself and the ways of man.

*

The partition of India and Pakistan took place in 1947 with the drawing of the Radcliff Line, a border drawn by an Englishman who had yet to visit the region. Over 10,000,000 were uprooted in what was perhaps the greatest exodus of the modern era. Widespread violence fueled the chaos, neighbors killing neighbors, old scores settled; the slaughter of travelers as they passed through anonymous villages. Historians estimate the death toll to have been at least one million. Like the slaughter a decade earlier of Haitian Creoles by the Dominicans, both parties shared the same geography and skin color, yet, unlike the Parsley Massacre, there was no secret code word to cue the butchering. So how did factions determine who was going to die? It was easy. They used the fairy tales they told themselves of how the world began and what would happen after they died.

Ever since, the subcontinent has been locked in its own bloody cycle. The first Indio-Pakistan War took place from October 1947 to December 1948, and the countries have rekindled hostilities in 1965, 1971, and 1999. Their shared border is considered as one of the tensest in the world. Both countries possess over one hundred atomic warheads, and some believe if each side unleashed their full arsenal, the world would be plunged into a Nuclear winter.

*

"Wherever morality is based on theology, wherever right is made dependent on divine authority, the most immoral, unjust, infamous things can be justified and established."

—Ludwig Feuerbach

*

YOU HAVE LITTLE TO EAT BUT A BODY GETS USED TO IT A CONSUMING OF FAT THEN MUSCLE A HUMAN FOOD AND WITHIN YOU A GLOW LIKE THE STARS THAT PRODUCE THEIR OWN FUEL AND YOU TREAD ACROSS THIS MOONSCAPE YOU AND THE OTHER BEATING HEARTS FLAWS IN THE DESIGN OF DEATH AND YOU'RE PUT TO WORK A CORPSE MINER THE UNEARTHING OF THOSE WHOSE STARSHINE HAS BEEN SNUFFED AND YOU CARRY THEM GRABBING FEET OR ANKLES OR SOLO IF IT'S A CHILD AND YOU STACK THEM IN PYRAMIDS LAYERS OF MEAT AND WOOD AND WHEN THE TORCH IS SET YOU TRY TO STAND DOWNWIND BUT IT'S IMPOSSIBLE THE FLAMES AND SMOKE SWIRLING THE FLICKERING LIGHT IN YOUR EYES

*

Another purchase at the Ardmore Bookstore—Ray Bradbury's collection *Golden Apples of the Sun*. My favorite story—"A Sound of Thunder." The story's premise—a time machine carries hunters into the past to kill dinosaurs, beasts that are destined to die within minutes of other causes. As the story begins, a hunter named Eckles and the other expedition members express their relief over the recent presidential elections, the victory of the sensible Keith over the fascist Deutscher.

The hunting party travels back. Their strict instructions —they can only shoot the designated animals, and above all, they can't leave the levitating path that separates them from the earth. The men encounter the selected T. Rex, but Eckles loses his nerve, and during his retreat, he stumbles off the levitating path.

Upon his return, Eckles discovers the world he left intact yet oddly warped. Skewed behaviors, words spelled differently. Then the news that Deutscher has defeated Keith. Eckles picks up the boots he wore on the safari. Caught in the muddy tread, a single butterfly.

One of the most popular sci-fi stories of all time, "A Sound of Thunder" also helped usher in the phrase "The Butterfly Effect." Rooted in chaos theory, Edward Lorenz proposed that a single flap of a butterfly's wings could trigger a ripple that could eventually alter the path of a hurricane. Scientists and mathematicians have developed models for chaotic motion. The main variables—initial conditions and the approximate return of a system to those conditions, which is also termed *recurrence*.

In *Treehouse of Horror V*, the Simpsons parody "A Sound

of Thunder." Homer accidently creates a time machine when he's trying to fix the toaster. He travels into the past, kills a mosquito, and returns to a world ruled by Ned Flanders.

"Hi-dilly-ho, slavereenos!"

*

H. G. Wells published *The Time Machine* in 1895. It was Wells who coined the term "time machine," and his novel is considered the first incarnation of mechanized, fourth-dimension frolicking in popular literature. The nameless Time Traveler skips hundreds of thousands of years into the future to discover a nightmare of divergent evolution. Our hero, chased by hideous mutants, flees. His machine whisks him millions of years into the future, a time when Earth is ruled by giant crabs and butterflies.

The Time Traveler returns to Victorian England. His friends believe he has only been gone for a few hours. They haven't changed—this is pre-Einstein, pre-theory of relativity after all.

How does our pilgrim's story end? We're not sure. Not long after his return, he disappears with his machine. He's seen so much. He doesn't want to be here anymore. He surrenders himself to the haze of time.

*

Wells' *The Time Machine* has been made into a full-length movie three times. Other films have employed Wells' invention to imagine the ramifications of time travel:

Back to the Future—can Marty McFly make his yet-to-be and unsettlingly hot mother fall out of love with him and hook her up with his father, thus ensuring his own birth?

The Terminator—can a future cyborg kill every Sarah Connor in the Los Angeles phonebook, a preconception abortion that will snuff out a future uprising led by Connor's unborn son, the rebel leader? Wait—the rebel leader is the child of the human sent back to protect Sarah Connor from the cyborg? How the hell does that work?

Donnie Darko—that rabbit! Good Lord, that rabbit!

Hot Tub Time Machine—it's all there in the title.

*

I became a so-called science fiction writer when someone decreed that I was a science fiction writer. I did not want to be classified as one, so I wondered in what way I'd offended that I would not get credit for being a serious writer. I decided that it was because I wrote about technology, and most fine American writers know nothing about technology. I got classified as a science fiction writer simply because I wrote about Schenectady, New York. My first book Player Piano, was about Schenectady. There are huge factories in Schenectady and nothing else. I and my associates were engineers, physicists, chemists, and mathematicians. And when I wrote about the General Electric Company and Schenectady, it seemed a fantasy of the future to critics who had never seen the place.

*

When I was in first grade, one of my favorite TV shows was *The Time Tunnel*. Every Friday night, right after *The Green Hornet*, I watched the adventures of time castaways Drs. Tony Newman and Douglas Phillips (their outfits always the same, reminders of their outsiders' status—Doug's neat, gray suit, Tony's mod turtleneck). The pair encountered danger at every turn, capture, imprisonment, the threat of death; their peril heightened by their knowledge of the near-future. On board the Titanic. Riding with General Custer. Standing at the rumbling base of Krakatau. Back in the Time Tunnel command center, Lt. General Heywood Kirk and Drs. Raymond Swain and Ann MacGregor worked tirelessly to rescue their comrades, often plucking them just in the nick of time before spitting them out in a distant loop of the fourth dimension, the next episode teased as Tony and Doug came to grips with their new realities.

Unlike Billy Pilgrim and the Tralfamadorians, Drs. Newman and Phillips were not passive visitors. They did their best to warn their supporting cast, but they often found themselves mocked. Custer's arrogance. The belief in an unsinkable ship. Altering the larger history was beyond the good doctors, but they sometimes helped steer minor players to safety. These people have already had their time; they're all dead. Yet they exist—if not in the doctors' time then at least in time itself. Complications set in, the complexities of the heart. Tony falls in love with Princess Serit, daughter of Kublai Kahn. In the Pearl Harbor episode, he encounters his father, a man about to be killed in the attack, and his own, younger self. Poor Tony—lost within both his present and his past.

Curious, I click a YouTube search. There are no episodes, but I find the opening credits. A hip animation that could pass as art, an angular silhouette captured in an hourglass, a burial in sand. The music an agitated arrangement, and within me, an unexpected triggering, a memory suddenly vivid. Our old living room. The black-and-white TV, the one with the perforated cardboard back, and inside, the orange of glowing tubes. The cable knit rug. Me sitting close, the anticipation of adventure.

*

Billy Pilgrim suffers. He carries scars not granted the body's luxury of healing. Wounds relegated to the dark, injuries he himself can't understand. His trauma tears a wormhole into an alternate reality, one where life's horrible events vanish with a diversion of the eyes. In a book filled with spaceships and time travel and telecommunicating aliens, the most outlandish element of Vonnegut's new order is the creation of a world without suffering.

The addressing and easing of suffering is a cornerstone of the world's major religions. Men of the cloth are fixtures on battlefields and in hospitals. Eulogies are one of the oldest forms of the oral tradition. Seeking comfort, we call to our gods in times of pain. For Christians and Muslims, worldly suffering pales beside the eternity of heaven's reward. In the Germanic pagan religion of Asatru, Valhalla is a special heaven for warriors killed in battle. There are 144,000 reserved spots in the VIP area of paradise for Jehovah's Witnesses.

Few belief systems tackle suffering as directly as Buddhism. The First Noble Truth is often translated into English as "life is suffering." Translation, especially from ancient texts, can be a tricky thing, and there are many in the Buddhist community who believe this interpretation doesn't do the First Truth justice. They point to the earliest scriptures and their use of the term *dukkha*. *Dukkha* proves a difficult word to pin down, a term that has no corresponding bull's-eye in English. They break down *dukkha* into three categories. *Dukkha-dukkha* addresses the traditional concept of suffering, pain of the physical and emotional varieties. There is *viparinama-dukkha*, the concept that there isn't much in this life that's permanent. Happiness is *dukkha*. Ecstasy is *dukkha*. Grief is *dukkha*. These states are fleeting; they will ebb and tide, a flow impossible to hasten or stall. Finally, there is *samkhara-dukkha* which, in its simplest form, reminds us that everything is connected—that the circumstances that impact us and our own actions and responses are all links in a greater chain. Suffering—impermanence—interdependence. We hurt. Neither our pain nor joy will last forever. We are all connected—our grief, our happiness. Listen and you will hear the flap of a billion butterfly wings.

Some have sought out suffering as an avenue to the divine. Good Friday in the Philippines brings reenactments of Christ's passion, men nailed or bound to crosses and hoisted into the warm air. Thomas Becket, St. Patrick, Henry the Navigator, St. Francis of Assisi, and other devout followers were known to wear hair shirts. The all-stars of self-imposed suffering were the Flagellants of the 14th century. Traveling in packs numbering in the thousands, the Flagellants roamed the European countryside, their ranks swelling in times of drought and disease. Their procession entered a town, God's word on their tongues. Some staggered beneath the weight of shouldered crosses. Others whipped themselves or their fellows with scourges featuring knotted leather strips, some fixed with nails. Blood flowed, wounds of rapture. The Flagellant movement reached its peak during the Black Death. The tribe suffered for penance and prayed for mercy. Modern researchers are powerless to assess penance and mercy, but they do agree the Flagellants aided the plague's spread.

*

From 1975–1978, the Khmer Rouge killed over 2,000,000, a quarter of Cambodia's population. Cities were emptied as their citizens were herded into the countryside, a disastrous attempt to establish an agrarian, Communist utopia. Teachers, professors, and civil servants were summarily executed. Also gunned down were those who wore glasses, which the revolutionaries considered a symbol of the bourgeois.

*

"And even if wars didn't keep coming like glaciers, there would still be plain old death."

Here is Vonnegut's lament in chapter one—a shrugging of shoulders, an admission of impotence. I have my own views on religion, meaning, life, and death. In the end, these beliefs amount to nothing. They are part of the light that shines for me alone. Then death. The light goes out. The flow stops.

I do my best to be kind, yet I fall short of the man I want to be. I keep trying, and what I fear is the day when that proves too much. I'm comfortable in my skin—it's one of the gifts of age—yet a child changes the equation. The other day my son asked what matters when we all end up dead? When our self-important history is recognized as a blip in the only slighter larger blip of our kind? He is my son after all, and even though I've never told him such a thing, he's a sensitive soul. Here's my response—you're right, my boy, little matters. Us, our time, our schemes and desires. And here's my response, part two—everything matters. Holding a door for the family behind us matters. Saying good morning to a hiker we pass on the trail matters. Calling your grandmother to tell her you love her matters. Trying your best on your homework matters. Kind words matter. Perseverance matters. Courage matters. Strength matters. Forgiveness matters. "Please" matters. "Thank you" matters. "I'm sorry" matters.

And here is what I'll tell my boy about death—that death is both forever and a single moment. That I know nothing about what waits beyond, a lack of understanding that's just another drop in a greater ocean of mystery. And while death is a moment, life is a richness of moments, each an opportunity to hold our lens just so, a tilting of perspective to see—beneath the layers of meaninglessness—the things that truly matter.

*

Kurt Vonnegut on semicolons: "Here is a lesson in creative writing. First rule: Do not use semicolons. They are transvestite hermaphrodites representing absolutely nothing. All they do is show you've been to college."

I'm not overly fond of the semicolon, but I do enjoy having it in my toolbox. I enjoy the semicolon's asymmetry, its unique place in the geeky pantheon of grammar; I enjoy its sense of borders and new starts in a long series; I enjoy the immediacy it provides in linking thoughts without a conjunction's interference.

Anyway, I've always had a soft heart for the misunderstood. You're OK with me, semicolon.

*

Listen:

Here's how the Tralfamadorians tried to explain their view of time to befuddled Billy Pilgrim—the Rocky Mountains seen all at once, a stretching vista of peaks, a breathtaking panorama.

Here's how they explained an earthling's conception of time—a man with a steel sphere encasing his head and welded to it, a peephole in the form of a long, open-ended tube. The human is then strapped into place and set in motion upon a flatbed railcar. The peephole's tiny aperture is the moment. The flatbed's turning wheels are the days of his life. Forward, forward, and the images flicker at the pipe's end until the wheels grind to a halt. The peephole closes. The ride ends. So it goes.

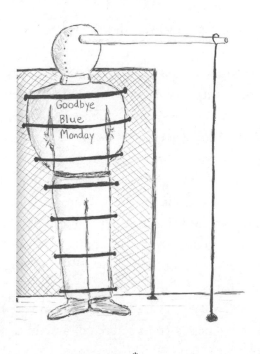

*

J. B. Dunlop's 1887 invention of inflatable tire tubes was a boon to the transportation age. The worldwide demand for rubber skyrocketed. This was wonderful news for King Leopold II of Belgium. Why? Because the Belgian Congo, a tract of land sixty-five times larger than Belgium itself, was rich not just with timber, ivory, and minerals, but also with groves of *hevea brasiliensis*. Or more commonly, the rubber tree.

Hooray for the filled coffers of Belgium! Hooray for King Leopold II and the public works and palaces built on the trade earned by the Congo! Hooray for the unbridled power of free enterprise!

The Congolese, however, didn't fare so well. Villages that didn't meet their quotas where subjected to retribution. Estimates place the toll of those murdered, starved, or worked to death at over 10,000,000. When putting down insurrections or dealing with stubborn natives, Belgian soldiers were under strict orders not to waste their bullets. To prove they weren't firing their guns willy-nilly, the soldiers harvested the right hand of each murdered victim. Thus began a new trade in the Congo, with both white soldiers and warring tribes dealing in the traffic of human hands, some hacked from the dead, others from the living, the hunters padding their tallies with the unfortunates who crossed their paths.

From 1898 to 1901, Alice Seely Harris and her husband served as missionaries in the Congo, and in a series of photographs, she exposed the atrocities she'd witnessed, most notably, pictures of men, women, and children whose arms ended in abrupt stumps. Harris published a book, and she and her husband toured England and the United States, spreading the news of the horrors she'd witnessed.

The reaction? A widespread revulsion—and Belgium's eventual ceding of the Congo. For once, the Tralfamadorian tradition of ignoring this world's unpleasant pictures went unheeded. Hooray for Alice Seely Harris! Hooray for mankind! Hooray for not averting our eyes!

*

The day after Vonnegut's death, Fox News broadcast a two-minute obituary. The report's veneer of respect faded quickly. Vonnegut after all had been vocal to the end about his distaste for the regime and the current conservative movement of Bible-thumpers and climate-change deniers. No mention was made of his military service or his Purple Heart. The report said that Vonnegut had been famous, but his "left-wing screeds" were "too quirky, too filled with scatological humor" to have him placed among the "great pantheon of American writers." *Slaughterhouse-Five* was a success, but "by the late 70s Vonnegut was rich and irrelevant . . . a sacred cow of the New York literary scene." They played a Charlie Rose clip where an aged Vonnegut said an author's best work was done by the time he was fifty-five, then the voiceover: "But Kurt Vonnegut kept at it and persisted in his unique brand of despondent leftism." They mentioned his failed suicide and a quote hoping his children wouldn't say of him: "He made wonderful jokes, but he was such an unhappy man." Then the voiceover: "So I'll say it for him." Pause. "Kurt Vonnegut was eighty-four."

I'd like to think Mr. Vonnegut gets the last laugh when

his readers come upon a passage in *Slaughterhouse-Five* attributed to Harold Campbell, the American playwright turned Nazi. In a manifesto about his ex-countrymen written for the Germans overlooking US POW's, Campbell reaches into the future and speaks to the soul of Fox News, the far right, and the one percent:

America is the wealthiest nation on Earth, but its people are mainly poor, and poor Americans are urged to hate themselves. To quote the American humorist Kin Hubbard, 'It ain't no disgrace to be poor, but it might as well be.' It is in fact a crime for an American to be poor, even though America is a nation of poor. Every other nation has folk traditions of men who were poor but extremely wise and virtuous, and therefore more estimable than anyone with power and gold. No such tales are told by the American poor. They mock themselves and glorify their betters. The meanest eating or drinking establishment, owned by a man who is himself poor, is very likely to have a sign on its wall asking this cruel question: 'if you're so smart, why ain't you rich?' There will also be an American flag no larger than a child's hand—glued to a lollipop stick and flying from the cash register.

Americans, like human beings everywhere, believe many things that are obviously untrue. Their most destructive untruth is that it is very easy for any American to make money. They will not acknowledge how in fact hard money is to come by, and, therefore, those who have no money blame and blame and blame themselves. This inward blame has been a treasure for the rich and powerful, who have had to do less for their poor, publicly and privately, than any other ruling class since, say Napoleonic times. Many novelties have come from America. The most startling of these, a thing without precedent, is a mass of undignified poor. They do not love one another because they do not love themselves.

*

So Kurt Vonnegut and I don't see eye-to-eye on the semicolon. Another point of contention—that a writer has done his best work by fifty-five. My second favorite Vonnegut novel is *Bluebeard*. It was published when he was sixty-five. Well into his seventies and eighties, he put out essays that I consider some of his wittiest and most honest work. As a man who's just turned fifty-five, I'm happy to disagree with this as well.

*

Actress Marilu Henner is among the slim demographic who possess what neurologists have termed Highly Superior Autobiographical Memory. Henner and those like her are able to recall their pasts in stunning detail. Given a specific date, they can tell the day of the week, the weather, what they wore and ate. They describe their memories as three-dimensional, the revisited past an experience so deep they remember the feel of their clothing. The taste of their food. The day's emotions.

MRI scans show those with Highly Superior Autobiographical Memory have blazed an active pathway between the brain's front and back. Dr. James McGaugh has studied this phenomenon. He theorizes this condition may be due to different parts of the brain having greater access to each other. Henner and those like her are able to almost relive the happiest days of their lives, a continual reunion with the things they have loved and lost.

And like Billy Pilgrim, they can never escape the worst moments either. Those of us with normally wired brains can cloud the past. We can bend its narrative, rationalizing, justifying, forgetting. We can tell ourselves we got a few good punches in during a fight that ended in humiliation. We can convince ourselves the horrible words we spoke to a friend weren't really so bad. While I'm fascinated by the condition of Superior Autobiographical Memory, I wouldn't like to possess it, and here is a lure of Tralfamadorian thought—the option of turning our gaze when faced with what monsters have done to us and when we, ourselves, have acted as monsters.

*

I have, in my time, for a brief period, dealt with an enormous number of bodies and seen these spectacular pyramids of corpses alternating with wood.

*

I did my best to fill my son's early years with words. Songs. Nursery rhymes. Talking, showing, explaining. Most of all, books—picture books, bright colors, friendly animals. Many with pages ripped, and by the time my son could speak, we were deep into our second and third copies of his favorites. *Drummer Hoff. Brown Bear. Frederick. Make Way for Ducklings.* On the lazy mornings of a teacher's summer, we'd carry our boy into our room, snuggling him between us, reading as the sun slanted across our bed. Years passed, and picture books gave way to longer stories, and a chapter at a time, we joined the adventures of *Stuart Little, Call of the Wild, Mrs. Frisbee and the Rats of NIMH.*

A confession: I'm not a great conversationalist. I tend to let others do the talking. I don't enjoy chatting on the phone. I like my banter light—jokes, a bit of self-effacement, a busting of balls. But before my son could ask a question of his own, I strove to fill his head with words—and as his knowledge of language grew, I offered him more stories, for a story presented aloud is a different experience for both reader and listener, not as private yet acutely intimate, a type of magic an adult can easily forget.

In my first decade of working with high school students, I taught, among other things, language arts. All my students had learning needs, my classes a mix—often a dozen or more, farm kids, motor heads, sad stories, tough girls—many at odds with the administration or the local cops. Together, we took little steps. Decoding strategies, word families, the use of context. Our progress was grudging, their fingers creeping beneath the printed words, their lips moving, the vexing soup of letters and sounds and punctuation. There were sighs and painful test scores and the realization I might just be smothering what little joy they still found in the process. So between units, or sometimes in their stead, I read to them. These were the pre-standardized testing days, the classroom mine to run, the curriculum nonexistent beyond keeping my crew out of the principal's office. I shared the newspaper. Poetry was a bust, but magazine accounts of crimes and natural disasters, the bloodier the better, always stirred discussion. What I remember most are the books. *Old Yeller. The Best Christmas Pageant Ever.* The stories of O'Henry. The simplified versions of *A Tale of Two Cities* and *Robinson Crusoe.* Some rolled their eyes, others put down their heads, but overall there was stillness, one of the rarer commodities in my room. Here was the quiet of engagement, and upon me, the gazes that had forgotten their hard stances, their hurt and frustrations.

As an adult, I too rediscovered the rewards of being read to. The advent of audiobooks, the box set of cassette tapes I borrowed from the library. The experience wasn't always perfect, but with the proper mix of material and narrator, I have been moved. The summer day my wife and I pulled over on a quiet Vermont road to hear Lenny and George's last conversation as the posse closed in. The cold night we listened to a passage from Anne Frank's diary, a tenderly worded insight that brought us to tears.

As I prepared for this book, I found a recording of *Slaughterhouse-Five* read by Ethan Hawke. Sometimes it's difficult to jibe a familiar book with a voice outside one's head, but I've been won over by Hawke. He brings no outside distractions. He seems like a decent person. He's done good work. He hasn't made an ass out of himself, which is more than I could have done had I spent the last twenty-plus years beneath Hollywood's magnifying glass. I listen in bed, headphones on, my day behind me and my body humming with fatigue. Sleep isn't far off, and I honor the spirit of Billy Pilgrim by randomly plunking myself into the text and pressing play. I listen, holding onto the images, feeling them in a different part of my brain, trying to see it all anew as I drift into dreams.

*

In 1818, the British occupiers in Sri Lanka faced a native uprising in Uva, a province in the Kingdom of Kandy. In what came to be known as the Uva-Wellasa Massacre, Governor Robert Browning gave the order, "Slaughter every man, woman and child, including babes suckling at the breast." His troops obeyed. The following year, Browning was promoted to a full general.

*

"It is forbidden to kill. Therefore, all murderers are punished, unless they kill in large numbers and to the sound of trumpets."   —Voltaire

*

I come down with the flu. All of my meaty parts ache. I grow dehydrated, my mouth parched but even a sip turns my stomach. The first night I don't sleep. The second night I drift, an hour at a time, and I'm not sure if I'm dreaming or hallucinating. The same narrative arcs through my brain each time I close my eyes. I have to fill out a form, but the questions continually change. I follow the form in and out of consciousness. The bed sheets dampen with sweat. Questions and answers turn on each other, punctuation melts away, and I'm left with a loop of words without beginning or end, and I, too, become part of the cycle, lost within its confusion. I grope the nightstand, looking for a pen, but is this searching just another dream? I think of Billy Pilgrim, lost in time, weaving in and out of the moment that is, only I lack his good humor, his grace. Instead, I'm agitated, my desire to shout hampered by my exhaustion, my raw throat. Near dawn, I see the questionnaire again, only now it's written on the yellow-white of scrambled eggs poured into a hot pan. The writing bubbles, and the words change again. The smell hits my nostrils. The imagined scent triggers a very real revulsion, a riot in my gut as I stumble into the bathroom.

*

If asked, I'll say this is my first memory: a flag-draped coffin, a horse-drawn cart. I'm three, and my TV shows aren't on today.

Another city, another living room, and in this cramped

space, I'll first learn of another Kennedy killed. And King. The moon landing. Nixon's resignation. The modern connection, images in black and white.

My junior year of college, and I heard about John Lennon during Monday Night Football. Fast forward five years and I witness the Challenger disaster with a classroom of eighth graders. Skip ahead four more years, and I watch the Berlin Wall come down.

I remember all these things. Or do I?

In 1977 Harvard researchers Roger Brown and James Kulik asked their study's participants the impact of such communal events and coined the term "flashbulb memory." Most respondents vividly recalled where they were when they heard the news from Dealey Plaza. From Warm Springs, Georgia. From the Lorraine Motel in Memphis. Many could recall the tableaux in captured detail—the air's scent, the clothes one wore. Flashbulb—the moment preserved. That rare intersection of one's personal narrative and history. Scientists eyed the amygdala, a region of the brain that grows more active with heightened emotions. An overlapping of input, a sense of shock. The bulb goes off; the observer and everyone around him caught in the light; the world, in some way, changed.

In the weeks after the 9/11 attacks, memory scientists began gathering New Yorkers and asking them a series of basic questions about the day. Follow ups occurred at regular intervals. One year. Two. Three. Those who'd witnessed the towers' fall anywhere south of Washington Square tended to retain a true, distinct recall as the years passed. But when the groups shifted to those who'd been at Midtown and north, the details of those initial memories assumed the same, fading trajectory as normal ones. The researchers guessed proximity might have fueled the already hyped amygdala. What was vivid for all of us would, for those closest to Ground Zero, shine even brighter.

Memory splinters further still. Consider the vagaries of emotion, our inability to extricate our feelings on a future date from the act of looking back. Then there are the false memories. Ones inescapable, the pictures the world shared—but did we experience them in the moment or later, in the fog that follows such an event, especially in these days of continual news coverage, the relentless bombarding of images? Did you wear your yellow shirt that day or was it that blue one, the one you always looked better in anyway?

Maybe I was reading a book the night Nixon resigned— or catching fireflies in the backyard in the last gasp of childhood. Maybe I didn't see John Kennedy's flag-draped coffin after all. I was there, yes, but perhaps the moment's framing isn't the solid thing I believed it was.

*

Billy Pilgrim was born on July 4, 1922. July 4th is, of course, Independence Day. Traditional American activities on July 4th include barbecues and fireworks. Billy Pilgrim died on February 13, 1976. 1976 was celebrated as the United

States' bicentennial. February 13th is the anniversary of the firebombing of Dresden, and there are still a few survivors who recall that night in 1945 with its gunpowder explosions and scents of charred meat.

*

In A-time, the movie of one's life only moves forward. Death waits in the final frame. There can be no other resolution.

In B-time, the projectionist can flip a switch, the cogs and sprockets turned back. The images dance, a returning to life. To innocence. To birth.

*

Billy Pilgrim shares his birthday with James Edward Baker, better known as Father Yod, leader of the Source Family commune. On the same day, Lothar von Richtofen, German World War I ace and brother of the famous Red Baron, died in a plane crash. February 13, 1976 saw the assassination of Nigeria's military ruler, Murtala Mohammed, but most Americans remember it as the day Dorothy Hamill, our wedge-coiffed sweetheart, skated to Olympic gold.

The film runs, forward and back. Hello! Farewell! Hello!

*

At their first POW camp, Billy Pilgrim and the other American POWs were greeted by a show-tune-singing contingent of British officers. A clerical error early in the war had placed the Brits among the continent's most well-off individuals, an extra zero on a Red Cross form, a ten-fold increase in their monthly rations. The officers had each attempted escape at least once, so to thwart future attempts, their camp was actually a tiny island in a sea of dying Russians. The Russians, sub-humans in Reich's eugenic hierarchy, were being slowly starved to death. The Germans adored their British prisoners—their high spirits, their impeccable manners, their style and vigor—so they never stopped their avalanche of supplies. The Americans arrived to the Brit's prepared feast and a night of bawdy theater. The Brits were quietly disappointed in their allies. They'd expected cowboys, heroes. What they got were undisciplined children, urchins half starved and dazed.

On his first night in the camp, Billy crumbled into a laughing fit so intense he had to be subdued with morphine. He drifted into an opiate sleep and dreamed of giraffes, creatures gentle and beautiful and perplexing. In the dark after midnight, woozy with drugs and time travel, he staggered outside to take a piss. He became disoriented then found himself entangled on a barbwire fence. On the Russian side of the fence, a man even more pathetic than Billy. The Russian helped free Billy. Then a glance. Dead eyes. A face of shadows and moonlight.

The British were cheery, rosy-cheeked. The kept up appearances. They were princes on their little island. Barbwire and armed guards and incredible fortune insulated them from the Russians. How could a soul stand to witness such horror? Old Epizelus went blind. The British simply turned off part of their brains, a collective blindness, and here waits the moral dilemma of our—and perhaps all—time. How can we, who've been given so much, justify ourselves in this world full of want?

The Tralfamadorians urged Billy Pilgrim to look at the pretty things, to ignore the troublesome, the ugly, the brutal. I can't accept this—yet I can't live without engaging in its practice. I fill the coffee maker each morning, rarely thinking about the multitudes who can only dream of clean water. I take the supermarket's stocked shelves for granted. I check labels, not wanting to support corporations who've chased cheap labor around the globe. I succeed at times, fail at others. I own an iPad. Nikes are the only running shoes I buy. I am little different than the prison-camp Brits, my mind on my own comforts, blind to the sweatshops of Malaysia and the electronics gulags of Chengdu, factories where workers barely older than my son toil, soldiers in another kind of children's crusade. Like Billy Pilgrim, I choose not too look too long at the faces beyond the wire.

Mary's anointing of Jesus is one of the few events that threads through all four gospels. The oil was expensive, three hundred denarii worth, a year's wages for a common laborer. A debate broke out among the disciples. Wasn't this wasteful? Judas the most adamant, and then Jesus' response. Mary was right to honor Him, her Lord. His time was short. The poor will always be with them, He said, but they wouldn't always have Him.

*

Billy Pilgrim drives a luxury car. He owns a beautiful house. Five optometrists work for him, a fortune made in frames. He owns holdings in hotels and Tastee-Freeze stands. He is a success, yet he is distant, a man surrounded by the stretching desert. He drives through the black part of town, his windows rolled up. He speaks to a military man at the Lion's Club, a major advocating bombing Vietnam back to the Stone Age. Billy, having walked through a city that had suffered such a fate, says nothing. He returns to an empty house. His wife and daughter gone for the day, his dog gone forever. He retreats to his bedroom and tries to sleep. He turns on his Magic Fingers bed, but the trembling massage brings no comfort. He begins to weep. His tears soft, mysterious, their origin unexplained. Billy cries for everything and everyone and the emptiness surrounding him.

His doorbell rings. He pulls aside the curtain. A cripple waits on his stoop, another across the street. Waiting down the block, their boss, a man in a fancy car. The cripples are tools in a magazine-selling scam. They are weak, exploited, peddlers of a product that doesn't exist. They are refugees, echoes of the Soviet-fleeing streams Billy encountered on frozen German roads. The rich man waits in his warm car. A pimp. A trafficker in lies and damaged flesh.

Even Billy Pilgrim, with his comfort of time unending, can't stop his tears. He remains behind his locked door, overwhelmed by the sadness of it all. The stories told over and over, the lessons never learned. He closes his eyes, and when he opens them, his tears are those born from an icy wind as he and his fellow POWs march through the German winter.

*

In 1980, Kurt Vonnegut was asked to speak on Palm Sunday. His text for the sermon: John's version of the anointing. Listen:

> Perhaps a little something has been lost in translation ... I would like to recapture what has been lost. Why? Because I, as a Christ-worshipping agnostic, have seen so much un-impatience with the poor encouraged by the quotation "For the poor always ye have with you'" ... If Jesus did in fact say that, it is a divine black joke, well suited to the occasion. It says everything about hypocrisy and nothing about the poor. It is a Christian joke, which allows Jesus to remain civil to Judas, but to chide him for his hypocrisy all the same. "Judas, don't worry about it. There will still be plenty of poor people left long after I'm gone."

Perhaps Judas is the voice in my head when I try to reconcile my affluence in this world of sweatshops and starvation. Perhaps Judas' words articulate the schism that can send us into tears as we hide from the cripples knocking at our doors.

*

In his first dip into the chaos of unlinear time, Billy Pilgrim returns to the womb, a dome every bit as sheltering as the one he'd find on Tralfamador. When Christians speak of being born again, they talk of delivery and salvation. A rescuing from darkness. Billy Pilgrim, although not a believer, was born again—twice. He climbed a narrow stairwell, rising from the underground womb that had kept him safe, and was reborn into a moonscape of death. Years later, he opened his eyes, covered with the Vermont snow and barely alive, a plane crash's only survivor. Surrounding him, the ski patrol, men with faces shielded by masks. They brushed the snow from Billy's face, and he muttered a word they couldn't understand.

"*Schlachthof-fünf.*"

Slaughterhouse-five.

Billy wants to return to the womb. Of course, of course.

*

Speaking of Judas—whatever became of him? Here are some ideas:

<u>Dante</u>—Ninth circle of hell, and in that circle's fourth and final round, a centerpiece in the spectacle, forever gnawed headfirst in Satan's gnashing teeth. Ouch.

<u>John Calvin</u>—Of course he went to hell. Predestination and all that. Although in an uncharacteristic softening, Calvin cited Judas' actions as part of God's larger plan. He was a pawn, a tool in the fulfillment of prophecy. Still, no dice on the heaven thing.

<u>Billy Graham</u>—Straight to hell. Sure, he committed suicide out of regret and shame, but feeling bad about what one's done isn't the same as repenting.

The Vatican—That's a head-scratcher. He could have pulled the old salvation switcheroo at the last moment. One never knows.

The Gospel of Barabbas—Take the old switcheroo and turn it up a notch because here's the skinny—Judas and Jesus traded places at the moment of betrayal. Yes! Jesus ascended to heaven, while Judas, who now looked so like Jesus that even Mary couldn't tell the difference, got nailed to the cross. Kind of like a biblical *Freaky Friday*.

*

So if Fox News and the current conservative movement eschew the writings of Kurt Vonnegut, who have they adopted as their literary flag-bearer? None other than Ayn Rand. Each summer, Supreme Court Justice Clarence Thomas invites his new law clerks to his home to watch and discuss *The Fountainhead*. Tea Party darling Paul Ryan gives all his interns copies of *Atlas Shrugged*. In a 2005 speech to the Atlas Society, Ryan claimed Ayn Rand was "the reason I got involved in public service, by and large" (an odd statement considering Rand's position on public service). These men and their far-right cohorts embrace Christianity. They talk openly of their faith and their relationship with Jesus. Of the 301 Republicans elected to the 114th Congress, only one doesn't identify himself as a Christian. So what gives with the following for Rand, a writer who labeled religion and its followers as insipid?

Who detested the notion of duty to one's community and country? Who hated Ronald Reagan, conservatism's patron saint? *The sense of freedom is what calls us,* Rand's followers might say. T*he belief in the power of the individual.*

I would counter that the current political embracing of Rand is firmly rooted in money, as in not wanting to pay taxes. Or in money, as in uninhibited, laissez-faire capitalism (look how rich it made King Leopold II!). Or in money, as in the core objectivist principle of pursuing only the good of one's self and not supporting programs to offer a hand-up to those born in society's lower classes.

Here's my fear: that in my country there exists a current more malevolent than Tralfamadorian indifference, a movement that sees the poor as lacking not in opportunities or good fortune but in fundamental decencies. These politicians march beneath Jesus' cross but their agenda has little to do with the Sermon on the Mount. They worship capitalism and Rand's objectivism. They tell the poor to lift themselves up, but they don't offer a hand. They speak to the rich in nods and whispers, and the money flows.

A good teacher loves his students, but he realizes some require more love than others. For these, he offers extra doses of encouragement and support. He provides a scaffolding, a structure meant to lift but not intended to be permanent. He helps them stand straighter, see further. Expand this vision, and here is the society in which I want to live. Here is the inference beneath Jesus' words. The poor will always be with us, their problems and sufferings never to be erased. This question is, what are the rest of us willing to do about it?

In the 1990s, many young Christians began to sport bracelets bearing the acronym WWJD. *What Would Jesus Do?* I'm not a believer, but I appreciate the bracelet's message, its invitation to pause and find one's better self before acting. Here's one thing I know Jesus did—when He came upon the moneychangers in the temple, He became enraged and chased them off. Many evangelicals believe Christ's return is imminent. If this is true, I've got to believe there are a few more tables that are going to be kicked over when He discovers the policies championed in His name.

*

"But he saw too that in America the struggle was befogged by the fact that the worst Fascists were they who disowned the word *Fascism* and preached enslavement to Capitalism under the style of Constitutional and Traditional Native American Liberty."   —Sinclair Lewis

*

THE NIGHTMARE ENDS AND YOU RETURN TO THIS PLACE YOU'D DREAMED OF AND WAITING IS THE HOUSE OF YOUR CHILDHOOD AND THE BACKDROP OF ALL YOU KNEW AND WERE AND YOU JOIN BACK IN AS IS EXPECTED AND YOU CONTINUE THE TRAJECTORY YOU'D ENVISIONED AND YOU BECOME AN ICE SKATER MOVING

FORWARD GLIDING GLIDING UNTIL THE DAY THE ICE CRACKS AND YOU CRASH INTO THE DARK AND EVERY BIT OF YOU IS WEIGHED DOWN AND PULLED TO THE BOTTOM AND YOU'RE TAKEN TO A BRIGHT ROOM AND YOUR MOTHER VISITS AND SHE BRINGS HER CHEERY WORDS AND THE MEMORY OF THE WORLD ABOVE THE ICE AND ITS GLIDING TRAJECTORY AND SHE TALKS AND TALKS BUT YOU CAN'T LISTEN AND YOU PULL THE COVERS OVER YOUR HEAD AND GIVE YOURSELF BACK TO THE DARKNESS

*

"In the councils of government, we must guard against the acquisition of unwarranted influence, whether sought or unsought, by the military-industrial complex. The potential for the disastrous rise of misplaced power exists and will persist.

"We must never let the weight of this combination endanger our liberties or democratic processes. We should take nothing for granted. Only an alert and knowledgeable citizenry can compel the proper meshing of the huge industrial and military machinery of defense with our peaceful methods and goals, so that security and liberty may prosper together."

—Dwight Eisenhower, farewell
address to the nation, 1961

*

As a child, I was fascinated by the larger wheels turning outside my world. I surveyed the newspaper, its gray smudge on my fingers. I flipped through our weekly deliveries of *Time* and *LIFE*. In elementary school, if I woke up early, I'd sneak downstairs and turn on the TV, the volume a whisper. I remember being alone on a warm June morning, the local programming taken over by the network to cover the shooting of Robert Kennedy. For a long time, I simply sat, enthralled and scared, trying to sort it all out before waking my parents. A ritual—our after-dinner viewing of the news—the black-and-white images from Vietnam and Prague, American ghettos and college campuses. I can still feel the pause that accompanied a news bulletin's interruption, my thoughts jumping ahead—*who's dead now?*

Important books are reflections of their times, and cast against the sixties' turbulence, *Slaughterhouse-Five* becomes even more vital. Vonnegut had fought the Nazis, but he conceded World War II was that rarest of creatures, a just war. Fascism's enslaving ideology and its corrupt eugenics. Human slaughterhouses. Death on an industrial scale. We committed our own atrocities, but ours were guided by better, if not perfect, angels.

Having witnessed the carnage done in the name of right, Vonnegut was vexed by Vietnam. He had gone to war to save the world from darkness. Now our young men were killing and dying in a conflict that should have meant little to us. We sank deeper, driven by forces that felt far removed from Main Street. A quagmire, the pundits said, an apt description that—in the evolving beauty of our language—would give way to the war's name itself, our future politicians united to avoid "another Vietnam." Still we fought and spent and died. The shadow of the military industrial complex crept across the country, and with its chill came the economics of unending global conflicts and the politics of militarism.

Eisenhower, a man who knew war, had warned us, and as the millennium turned, his farewell address had become prophecy. In Vonnegut's last few interviews, I've detected a weary sag to his voice. Age of course, the cigarettes he both loved and hated, the deterioration of the body, but I can't help thinking he'd begun to question the element of hope that had run beneath the chaos and absurdity of his work. He'd been forced to live through one last war, a war sold on lies, the military industrial shadow now darker, each Tomahawk missile costing over a million dollars, the price of a new school, a fund that could have sent a hundred poor teenagers to college. Vonnegut was exhausted by a political climate that had wrapped up patriotism with religion. That had broken unions and shrunk the middle class and cuddled up with Wall Street, all the while chastising the poor for being poor. I rewatch one of his later interviews. He sighs, shakes his head. Perhaps he's looking back and wondering what his generation had sacrificed so much for.

*

The last thing I ever wanted was to be alive when the three most powerful people on the whole planet would be named Bush, Dick, and Colon.

*

Inside the Tralfamadorian spaceship, Billy Pilgrim asks a simple question. "Why me?" The response: "That's a very *Earthling* question to ask, Mr. Pilgrim. Why *you?* Why *us* for that matter? Why anything?"

Christian and Jewish sermons on individual suffering often reference the Book of Job. A man of faith and good fortune, Job is made a pawn in a wager between God and Satan. Job loses his home, his possessions, his beloved children. Disease ravages his body. He suffers like no other man, and in the cruelest twist, his belief, solid and strong, is the reason for his torment. At his lowest point, he curses the day he was born, yet he never curses his God.

I'm a believer in science, in the randomness of life, in the chaos theory and the butterfly effect, in the tumbling of a million crazy dominoes over which I have no control. I'm also an adherent to the power of free will and ownership, and here, in the delicate balance of one's decisions and the world's nonsensical cacophony, waits my life. This day. This moment. My life has been a run of good luck. Or perhaps this is only perception, a vision rooted in an underlying fatalism that my own suffering is biding its time.

When it comes to the contemplation of human pain, I can understand the appeal of religion. There's Buddhism, its assurance that one's suffering isn't earned, rather it's just another part of the process, the grinding of life's wheel. There's the Old Testament's Job and his conviction that God's wisdom wasn't for him to understand. There's Christianity, its purest reassurance found not in its scriptures or its promises of heaven—but in its sacrifice of God's only son, a fate as horrible as any man's.

Billy's "Why me?" is echoed later, a time slip back to the war. A fellow POW mutters something a guard doesn't like. The guard knows English, and he pulls the American out of ranks and slugs him in the mouth. The prisoner stands, spitting teeth and blood. He'd meant no harm. "Why me?" he asks the guard. The guard shoves him back into line. "Vy you?" the guard asks. "Vy anybody?"

Perhaps "Why me?" isn't the right question. Perhaps the right question should be "Why not me?" The shooting spree, the interstate pileup, the stage-four diagnosis, the fall from the ladder—I can't help but hear of these and wonder, *Why not me?* I think of Kilgore Trout's story, the outcast adopted by God as he hung on the cross, and the tale's lesson that we should never persecute "a bum who has no connections."

Here is the beauty of "Why not me?" *Why not me* removes us from survivor's relief, the ignoring of the bull's-eye we carry on our hearts. *Why not me* allows us a connection to the bums of the world who have no connections. *Why not me* brings us closer to the notion of brotherhood, of oneness, of identifying with rather than differentiating ourselves from the latest nobody nailed to a cross.

*

I think about my education sometimes. I went to the University of Chicago for a while after the Second World War. I was a student in the Department of Anthropology. At that time they were teaching that there was absolutely no difference between anybody. They may be teaching that still. Another thing they taught was that no one was ridiculous or bad or disgusting. Shortly before my father died, he said to me, 'You know—you never wrote a story with a villain in it.' I told him that was one of the things I learned in college after the war.

*

Vonnegut is too clever to make Paul Lazaro our villain. Lazaro is a sociopath, a man who projects his torment in acts of oddly justified violence. Despite this, he's just one man, and in a setting as brutal as war-torn Germany, there's little to differentiate him from a countryside crawling with killers.

If there is a villain, Billy meets him much later. Having survived a plane crash, Billy is rushed to a Vermont hospital where he shares a room with Harvard history professor Bertram Copeland Rumfoord. Brash, macho, and opinionated, a world-class sailor and author of a book on sexual vigor for older men, Rumfoord is recuperating from a skiing accident, and his new bride, a woman a third his age, brings him books for his research. He's a retired brigadier general in the Air Force Reserve. Rumfoord's current project is a study of the US air war in World War II. Poor

Billy stumbles through consciousness and time. Rumfoord detests Billy for his weakness, resents sharing his room with a man he considers a vegetable. Rumfoord and his trophy wife discuss the Dresden bombings. Rumfoord curses the soft hearts who've bemoaned the operation, a conversation Billy interrupts with three slurred words. "I was there."

In time, the men come to an understanding. They share a room after all, a generation, military service. Rumfoord softens, and he defends the Dresden attacks in civil tones. The horribleness of war. The evil of the Nazis. The sad duty of the men who flew the planes. All of it terrible, the men agree— Rumfoord believing it had to be done; Billy believing it was done and always would be done, inescapable and forever.

Here is our villain. Not Rumfoord—Vonnegut is quick to forgive us human types—but the ideas and rationalizations Rumfoord held as truths. In this sense, Rumfoord too becomes unstuck in time, for what he defends radiates beyond Dresden, a harkening back to all massacres and the justifications made by the victors and the writers of history. Educated, intelligent, well-spoken, Rumsfoord is the most dangerous of creatures, the respected man, a true believer who uses his gifts to convince us he knows what is right. That the horrible was justified. That the shedding of blood was, ultimately, proper and necessary.

*

Billy Pilgrim. I imagine Vonnegut took great care choosing the name. Drunk at a New Year's party, Billy cheats on his wife for the first and only time. The woman sits on a basement dryer, and as Billy helps remove her girdle, she asks, "How come they call you Billy instead of William?"

"Business reasons," Billy answers, his response short—there is business of another variety to attend to after all. But Vonnegut steps in and offers a deeper explanation. Billy's father-in-law's belief that "Billy" would stick in people's memories, a name "slightly magical, since there weren't any other grown Billys around." Billy—a child's name. Billy—a man defined by his war experiences, a child in a children's crusade.

Pilgrim. One who wanders. One who seeks, hoping to claim a better lot. His unique perspective of the fourth dimension turns Billy into a nomad within his own life. Billy first becomes time-spastic as he's lost and freezing behind German lines. He hears the womb's bubbling song, sees death's violet light. He returns to being a child, a boy picked up by his father and cast into a pool's deep end. Sink or swim, Billy-boy.

Childhood, the journey's beginning, and I think not of myself but of my son. He is on his own journey, and even when I'm by his side, he is still, at the deepest level, alone. Unlike Billy or Marilu Henner, my own childhood memories are sketchy, and what, I wonder, will my son remember? My quiet? My anger? My exasperation? My love?

My own journey is nearing its end, and when my son reaches my age, I'll be long gone. What do I wish for my child at the start of his own pilgrimage? Nothing more than the gifts I enjoy today. Health. Passion. Peace. Engagement. A hand to hold and a forehead to kiss at the end of a long day. What greater reward could a pilgrim ask for?

*

My parents and grandparents were humanists, what used to be called Free Thinkers. So as a humanist I am honoring my ancestors, which the Bible says is a good thing to do. We humanists try to behave as decently, as fairly, and as honorably as we can without any expectation of rewards or punishments in the afterlife. My brother and sister didn't think there was one, my parents and grandparents didn't think there was one. It was enough that they were alive.

*

The Tralfamadorians experience the fourth dimension not as a moment's thin slice but as a pool that starts at one's birth and runs as deep as their death. When they attempt to explain this to Billy Pilgrim, they rely on visual imagery. They encourage Billy to imagine the Rocky Mountains and a man strapped into a torture device, his head encased in steel, a single peephole through which to filter the world. (I'm repeating myself, aren't I? Help me, Billy—I, too, am becoming lost within my own narrative.)

It's no mistake the Tralfamadorians used pictures to convey their notions. Vision is our dominant sense. Our gifts of acuity and depth were honed on the planes of Africa and the ice-age forests of Europe. We saw our enemies and prey from a distance. We attacked or escaped. We survived. It's also no mistake Billy Pilgrim was an optometrist. He spent his days dealing with the eyes and perception. In his office, he helped others to see, and sometimes, in the examining room's dark, he wept, understanding the gift and pain of vision.

Seeing might be believing, but vision isn't truth. Ryūnosuke Akutagawa's short story "In a Grove" was the basis for Akira Kurosawa's classic *Rashomon*. The movie involves a rape and murder told through the eyes of four different players. The term "Rashomon Effect" addresses the phenomenon of individual perception in the often-slippery notion of truth.

Sight—like Vonnegut himself—is a trickster. Magicians and sleight-of-hand artists rely on our allegiance to vision. The avalanche of sight, the endless stimulus of the modern world, numbs us. There's simply too much to process. This ability to shut out and select might be what separates us from those with severe autism or schizophrenia or the LSD-trippers who can't stop their brains' colored flow.

If twenty of us were to stumble upon a scene of chaos, we could come away with twenty different truths. Police detectives might consider this aspect of human nature frustrating, but I can't help but be reassured. We feel. We think. Our memories aren't snapshots—they're collages pieced together to please an audience of one.

*

The Rashomon Effect has filtered its way into popular TV fare. In episode 15 of season 8, the guys of *Happy Days* are visiting Potsie's uncle's hunting cabin when the Fonz gets shot right through his favorite jeans' back pocket. At the hospital, each boy offers his unique version of the accident. Richie Cunningham, off at college, is spared the indignity of a half-hour of butt jokes.

In "Friend or Foe," the season five premier of *SpongeBob SquarePants*, Mr. Krabs shares the origin of his feud with Plankton. Plankton arrives and offers his own scenario of how the two, once partners and friends, became mortal enemies. Karen, Plankton's wife, offers the truth only a robot could deliver—that each were equally to blame for the dispute, and then offers the further revelation that the coveted Krusty Patty recipe was a fluke, the result of spices knocked from the kitchen shelf after an exiting Plankton slammed the door. There's a brief moment of reconciliation before Plankton attempts to steal the recipe again. Mayhem ensues.

*

"Poo-tee-weet?"

Here is *Slaughterhouse-Five*'s final line. A bird's question that punctuates a denouement of less than three hundred words, a passage that magically spans the lowest and highest points of Billy's journey. The passage begins with a destroyed Dresden. Billy becomes a corpse miner, the builder of colossal, human pyres. He works with a POW who dies of dry heaves after being forced to retrieve liquefying bodies. We're reminded of the fate of poor Edgar Derby.

Then in the next paragraph, deliverance. Spring and warmth. The corpse mines closed, the city's smoke scattered on the breeze. The Germany army gone to fight the advancing Russians. The POWs wake up one morning unguarded. The war over. Billy finds the abandoned horse cart he and his fellows will ride across the countryside, the wagon in which he will later have his life's most pleasant memory. The sun on his face and the knowing he's survived.

A bird calls. *"Poo-tee-weet?"* and a question mark makes all the difference, an asking neither Billy nor we can understand. A question without an answer beyond the understanding that our pilgrimages will be marked with incredible sorrows and joys. The understanding that so much is beyond our comprehension. That pain will find us and pass, and that happiness will do the same.

"Poo-tee-weet?" the birds ask. *"Poo-tee-weet?"*

*

In a hundred-day period in 1994, between 500,000 and 1,000,000 Tutsis were killed by their rival Hutus in Rwanda. Much of the initial killing was done by the army, police, and local militias, but once the blood started flowing, many civilians joined in. Most victims were cut down with machetes or clubbed to death. Some of the more compassionate killers offered the Tutsis the opportunity to purchase a bullet to shorten their suffering.

*

Guillermo del Toro, director of *Pan's Labyrinth* and *The Devil's Backbone*, has expressed his desire to shoot his own version of *Slaughterhouse-Five*. With a bit of luck, Billy

Pilgrim will return to the screen, cycled through to a new generation. The author dead. His story living on.

*

I take an online quiz—*What Was Your Past Life According to Your Memories?* I answer questions about first recollections and déjà vu, my parents, my first kiss.

My result—I was an inventor! I'm compared to da Vinci, Edison, Franklin. I'm told I'm ahead of my time. A radical who can change the world. My possibilities, I'm assured, are endless.

I take the quiz again, this time choosing the exact opposite answers. My result—pirate!

*

For argument's sake, let's separate writers into two camps. On one side, those who tell their stories, and on the other, those who tell our stories, the communal tales of mankind. Given these flawed choices, I'll put Vonnegut in the latter camp. True, he and Billy Pilgrim endured similar wartime experiences, but *Slaughterhouse-Five* transcends into a story of all struggles—soldier and civilian, prisoner and victor, a crumbling nation and death on every border. Vonnegut steps back and offers us a mirror. He invites us closer. "Look," he beckons.

He offers us sublime gifts. The wonders of chance and irony, the randomness of our days. We laugh at ourselves, the follies and vanity of men. Our hearts warm when we witness the good of which we are capable. We feel the sunshine upon our faces and the post-coital bliss of lying next to our spouse.

Then a twist. The mirror shifts, and here is another view. The cynical. The offensive. The wars. The massacres. The justifications of the powerful. The following of sheep. The sufferings of the weak. The Tralfamadorian indifference of those who refuse to act.

Another tilt, a final glance, and the image burrows deeper. An exposure of ourselves and our motivations. We're reminded that just as humanity is cruel, there is cruelty in the humane. We are all brothers and sisters, the carriers of beautiful flaws, and Vonnegut's isn't the only mirror. I think of Billy Pilgrim crying softly in his dark examination room, perhaps with the realization that there are mirrors everywhere, reflections carried in the eyes of every man, woman, and child.

*

Vonnegut's mirror addressed the duality of human nature. More obvious examples include:

Harvey "Two-Face" Dent—arch enemy of Batman. Half his face disfigured, acid thrown, and his life changed in an instant. He carries a coin, and with a flip, he decides his course of action—good or evil.

Janus—the Roman god of beginnings and transitions. One face turned forward, the other back. A god worshipped at planting time and harvests, weddings and funerals.

His gaze infinite, acute enough to look back over seasons. The course of a man's life. The time of all men.

Dr. Jekyll and Mr. Hyde—the doctor good, successful, but within, a constant battle, the suppression of urges. The potion he takes to battle his demons backfires. He changes, giving in to his dark callings, his body twisting and hardening. He becomes Hyde, wicked and hideous, and, in the end, stronger than his host.

The Hulk—the alter ego of mild-mannered scientist Bruce Banner, a transformation stirred by rage. His pained roots deep. An abusive father. A child who never overcame his fear.

*

My freshman psychology teacher drew on the chalkboard. An iceberg, only a fraction above the waterline. Below, the subconscious. Hidden. Vast. Mysterious. Here was where we'd buried our secrets. Our terror. The desires that spoke to us in the twisted language of dreams.

The iceberg model plays into the role of the Social Contract Theory. The repression of the Id necessary in a functioning society. Rules established and adhered to. We're raised—if we're lucky—to think before we act. We're introduced—if we're lucky—to a belief system that invites us to view a stranger as a brother. We are taught—if we're lucky—to be good boys and girls.

Then war, and in an instant, the structure of civilized society falls away. A nation's children are marched into the chaos. They are told to forget their saviors' messages of love. They are ordered to kill. They will never be the same. I think of the wars of my lifetime. Unfamiliar languages, the enemy who looks like a civilian. The women and children and no one to be trusted. A landscape of ghostly morals. The trigger squeeze that could be deliverance or murder.

A bomb goes off. In Dresden. Tokyo. Hanoi. Mosul. The shock wave hits, a pulse stronger than a hundred heavyweight punches. Eardrums cave, and the body's hollow parts—lungs, intestines, sinuses—act as echo chambers, and hidden from the eye, the swelling and bleeding begin. The flash burns exposed skin. Heat singes the throat, and what was solid a moment ago turns molten. Limbs are severed, bones broken. Tissue ripped. Lacerations scar the brain and liver. Those not already dead stagger from the smoke, coughing, blind. I think of Billy Pilgrim's backwards movie, and I wish I could whisk them all back in time, to high school. To when then they were babies. I think of Vonnegut stepping from his shelter and realizing he was part of the slaughter. His side. His cause. He didn't have to guess what waited in the iceberg's submerged mass. He saw it with his own eyes. He smelled it on the breeze. He felt it in his grip as he carried another corpse.

Then the other face. The many who go to war and behave honorably. Those who adhere to the codes they've been taught. Those who engage prisoners and civilians with empathy and compassion. Vonnegut gives us poor Edgar Derby, a man who never lost his faith in the rightness of the war and what America stood for. Derby epitomized the moral center that can survive the nightmare. His death—ironic, meaningless—is Vonnegut's lament. The sad truth that even the best of men are powerless against the maelstrom.

I've been asked in interviews if there is any common theme that runs through my work, and if I have to pick one, it would be the struggle to be good when being good is its only reward. A hard enough battle for any man—now consider the children who've returned from war. We've forced them to live through a nightmare. We tell them to turn off the switch and leave all that behind. We might as well ask them to run the movies of their lives backward. We might as well ask them to be babies again.

*

The Many-Worlds Interpretation comes to us from the sometimes counter-intuitive logic of quantum mechanics. Picture the pachinko machine, the shiny ball bouncing this way and that, an erratic yet singular route from start to finish. When the ball has come to a rest, run your own backward movie and see its path as a crooked silver line, a haphazard veering from obstacle to obstacle. Here is life, each deviation a reaction or decision, an image that resembles a lightning bolt arcing across the night sky. Now imagine that lightning bolt sharing its origin with a hundred thousand other bolts, these bolts dimmer but still real. Here is the same life, but with it, all of its alternate histories, the decisions unmade, the fortunes and tragedies avoided. The Many-Worlds Interpretation acknowledges that the initial, brighter lightning bolt constitutes one's reality, yet the whole, shining sky is also real, each bolt telling its own story not of what *might have been* but what *is* from a dimension beyond our understanding.

Now a new theory is sparking debate in the quantum mechanics community. The Many Interacting Worlds hypothesis suggests that not only are we surrounded by parallel realities, but that these narratives interact with ours, at least at the quantum level. The followers of science, so fond of empirical data, perk at this notion, for a mingling on the quantum level might just be detectable. The lightning bolts tangle, the sky alight, and it becomes impossible to tell where one world ends and the next begins.

*

Quantum mechanics, with its alternate and parallel realities, is based upon the Uncertainty Principle, which scientists have modeled with the formula:

$$\sigma_x \sigma_p \geq \frac{\hbar}{2}$$

where the standard deviation of an object's position and the standard deviation of its momentum are greater than or equal to the reduced Planck constant divided by two.

Heisenberg, bitches!

*

The movie industry might not understand the advanced calculations of the Uncertainty Principle, but they have had no trouble embracing its theories. Consider:

Sliding Doors—Gwyneth Paltrow narrowly misses her train … or does she? Her life splits into two parallel universes, one in which she catches the train, the other in which she doesn't. Neither life is particularly sunny, sorry to say. Sometimes happiness just isn't in the cards, kids.

Run Lola Run—Lola has twenty minutes to find 100,000 marks to save her mobster-hunted boyfriend. Three times she runs through Berlin. Common threads weave through the scenarios, yet each journey reaches a radically different conclusion. Death, salvation, reunion—each is likely as the other. Lola runs, possessed, unflagging, an orange-haired, boot-wearing force of will battling the mysteries of chance.

It's a Wonderful Life—George Bailey's suicide attempt is thwarted by Clarence, his guardian angel. George, like Job, wishes he'd never been born. This gives Clarence an idea. He takes George on a tour of what might have been, and the landscape ain't pretty. Like Clarence, we have to agree George really has led a wonderful life.

*

"The ball is round, the game lasts ninety minutes, everything else is just theory."

—German football legend Sepp Herberger

*

A new study from UCLA proposes a genetic link increases the likelihood of PTSD. For over twenty-one years, Dr. Armen Goenjian worked with survivors of the 1988 earthquake in Armenia that killed more than 25,000. His discovery—PTSD was more common in those who carried two gene variants—one which degrades dopamine and another which controls the production of serotonin.

Perhaps those old-time doctors were right. It really is all in our heads.

*

Freshman Psych, part 2—the nature vs. nurture debate, and I was a Henry Higgins man. Of course environment was the key. Privilege, exposure, education—these were the influences that shaped our human clay. I remain in the nurture camp, but now I hedge my bets. There is truth to the notion "born that way." Our genetic soup steeps inside us, a recipe we can never change. I believe in the tabula rasa, but not all blank slates are the same.

Nature and nurture—consider them the x and y coordinates on the human graph. Now add another dimension, a z-axis of a force beyond our earthly comprehension. Fate—the concept has been with us forever. Fate called the world's conquerors and explorers. Fate lay at the cornerstone of Calvinism's predestination. Napoleon Bonaparte claimed, "There is no such thing as accident, it is fate misnamed." One might think us modern types, this generation of self-actualization and technological miracles, would have abandoned notions of fate, but consider our terminal and happy weakness, the calling of love. A Marist poll shows over 75% of those under the age of forty-six believe in the existence of a soul mate, a singular, fated love meant to be ours.

Add Billy Pilgrim to those who believe in fate. For Billy, there is no free will, no quantum mechanics that would unravel the rope of his life into a thousand strands. There is only fate, his destiny pulling him like a magnet along the mysterious z-axis.

*

As Lola charges through the streets, "Believe" by Franka Potente plays:
I don't believe in pain
I don't believe there's nothing left
but running here again.

*

According to Pew research, over 1/3 of all Americans believe their lives are determined by forces outside their control. Another poll found that 1/4 of Americans believe God plays a role in determining the winner of the Super Bowl.

*

Joshua Oppenheimer's 2012 documentary *The Act of Killing* sheds light on the Indonesian genocide of 1965-66. Death squads, encouraged and supported by the military and police, fanned through the major cities. Communists were the primary victims, but other targets fell in the bloodlust— intellectuals, ethnic Chinese, Christian clergy. Estimates place the death toll between 500,000 and 1,000,000.

Oppenheimer employed a twisted frame, the executioners stars in a movie of their lives, the men taken back in time, their gray dyed away, makeup on their faces. The film drifts into the surreal, the old men turned young, the murderers revisiting their crimes, a shifting of perspective when they're forced to consider the eye of both the camera and of God. The movie starts with the men confident, but as they shoot the backward movie of their lives, some of the killers are left shaken, victims of their own trip through the years.

*

"Every gun that is made, every warship launched, every rocket fired, signifies in the final sense a theft from those who hunger and are not fed, and those who are cold and not clothed."   —Dwight Eisenhower

*

The goal of China's Great Leap Forward was to modernize China's economy. Industry would be stimulated, farms collectivized. Estimates place the movement's death toll between eighteen and thirty-five million. Most were claimed by famine that resulted from the program's disastrous policies, but at least two million were murdered, the powers that be seizing the opportunity to silence political opponents. Chairman Mao, addressing the 1959 Communist Party Congress, took responsibility for the program's failings by offering this apology: "The chaos caused was on a grand scale, and I take responsibility. Comrades, you must all analyze your own responsibility. If you have to fart, fart. You will feel much better for it."

*

Vonnegut wrote America's greatest gift to the world wasn't flight or the cheeseburger or the splitting of the atom—it was Alcoholics Anonymous, which offered those down on their luck a family that understood and accepted them. He also wrote about a baby born in an African village, an infant luckier than its American cousins despite its country's poverty and lack of material goods. Why was this child so fortunate? Because it belonged not just to its parents but to an extended clan of hundreds. He wrote about the difficulties of an American married couple and a wife's lament that her husband simply "wasn't enough people."

This belief in the importance of community might seem odd for a writer. We tend to be solitary types, our labors at our desks, wanderings made in silence, the search for meaning in the desert. But Vonnegut was offered one of history's rarest perspectives, the opportunity to walk across a decimated landscape, a man neither victim nor victor. Or more precisely, a man who was both. I can see him, his blank expression mirrored by his captors and fellow prisoners. Here might have been the seed of Vonnegut's yearning for a wider community, the belief that the more faces one knew and loved, the harder it would be to kill a stranger.

*

YOU CAN'T LIVE FOREVER BENEATH THE ICE AND IT'S NOT YOUR TIME TO DIE NOT YET SO YOU RISE TO THE SURFACE AND REJOIN YOUR TRAJECTORY AND YOU WORK AND MARRY AND HAVE SUCCESS AND CHILDREN AND TO THE WITNESSES YOUR LOT IS ENVIABLE ALL THE THINGS YOU'VE DONE AND POSSESS BUT THEY DON'T KNOW THE COLD BENEATH THE ICE THE PLACE YOU SLIP TO BETWEEN THOUGHTS A JOURNEY OF A SINGLE HEARTBEAT THE COLORS SO DARK AND HERE WAIT THE PYRAMIDS YOU MADE IN A DISTANT LAND AND A DISTANT TIME AND THE FIRES THAT WARMED YOUR CHEEKS AND THE SMOKE THAT STILL SINGES YOUR THROAT

*

The US soldiers of Vietnam fought a different war than their fathers. The enemy that struck and then melted back into the jungle. The protests back home. The lack of a definitive answer to the question: "Why are we here?" The exclusion of the upper classes, a segregation that would only escalate in the coming decades. Of the three million who served in Vietnam, an estimated 500,000 suffered from what came to be known as Post-Vietnam Syndrome.

58,209 US servicemen and women died in Vietnam. 153,303 were wounded. The rest came home to a conflicted country. The cold shoulder extended to the Veteran's Administration and their policy of denying claims of psychological damage that were made after six months of a soldier's return. In what areas did Vietnam vets enjoy a leg up on their non-fighting peers? According to the VA, it's in their higher rates of divorce, suicide, alcoholism, and drug addiction, that's where.

*

The Zimbardo Time Perspective inventory was designed to assess individual differences in the perception of time. The inventory's focus—an evaluation of the most pressing factors that influence one's decisions and actions. On a five-point scale ranging from Very Untrue to Very True, participants are offered scenarios such as *Painful past experiences keep being replayed in my mind* and *It upsets me to be late for appointments* and *Fate determines much in my life.*

Zimbardo used the responses to assign scores in five categories. There is the past-oriented person, a grouping then divided into past-negative and past-positive. Those who score high in this group tend to focus on obligations. They lean toward the conservative and are less likely to embrace the new or take risks. Those with higher past-positive scores are steady rollers; they possess a sense of community and nostalgia for their youth. Those with higher past-negative scores store up their disappointments and failures and traumas and use them to dampen the moment's joy.

The present scale is split into the present hedonistic and present-fatalistic. Present-hedonistic types enjoy the moment but are apt to be impulsive and reckless. Present-fatalistic people believe their fates are out of their hands. For them, there is no use in planning ahead since so much is beyond them. They struggle with depression and the negative spirals of self-fulfilling prophecies.

The final cluster addresses one's views of the future. Future-oriented folks tend to be reasonable and logical. They are capable of delaying gratification and see the benefits of long-term planning. They are retirement savers and exercisers and solid citizens. These positive qualities are balanced by their difficulties in being able to let loose and enjoy themselves. Their desire for control can make them a less-than-ideal partner for long-term relationships. The can come off as aloof.

I take the test. My scores—I land in the 50th percentile for both past-positive and past-negative; 10th for present fatalistic and 1st for present-hedonistic (I told you I was no fun at parties!); and 80th for future.

I channel the spirit of Billy Pilgrim and try again. My/his results—past-negative 80th percentile, past-positive 20th percentile. Present-fatalistic 99th percentile (of course). Present hedonistic 1st percentile (perhaps Billy and

I would hang together in party's lonely corner). Future—smack dab in the middle.

*

US troops invaded Afghanistan in 2001 and Iraq in 2003. Gone were Vietnam's jungles, replaced by dirt and sand, veins of lush river valleys and barren horizons. Rocky hills. A thousand dusty villages. Yet much remained similar to the previous generation's Vietnam. The hit and run of guerilla warfare. The conflicts' lack of a moral core. A fighting force disproportionately comprised of the lower and middle classes.

According to recent studies, roughly 25% of veterans returning from Iraq and Afghanistan have received mental health treatment from the VA. This percentage is more or less in line with previous wars with one difference—the incidences of stress disorders are being reported earlier, with most coming within a year or two after discharge. Some experts believe this trend may be due to an increased awareness and sensitivity to the onset symptoms of PTSD.

I think of nuclear weapons and our nearly seventy-year reluctance to use them again. Perhaps our view of the individual soldier is changing as well. Perhaps we're finally coming to grips with the human toll beyond the battlefield's wounds. Perhaps we're realizing that even if our sons and daughters return from war, they'll never be the same.

Or perhaps I'm no different than Alfred Nobel. Naïve in my hope. Ignorant in my wishes that man is capable of rewiring an instinct as old as history itself.

*

Billy Pilgrim has revisited the womb, the warmth and red glow. Fast forward fifty-four years, and he's experienced his death, the hum and purple light of his human machine shutting down. His unique view of time leaves him without fear. His death will be. His death is. His death was. Always and forever, hello and farewell.

As a child, I often imagined my own death. Certainly this is a common fantasy. Or maybe I was a morbid boy. Our days are a gift, but a child can't appreciate a gift given so easily. I viewed death as an act, the central drama from TV shows and movies. A role distant yet one which I was destined—someday—to play. These imaginings took place at night, in a bedroom's dark. The day's activity winding down. A child assumed to be drifting.

The script of my death was heroic. Romantic. I died for a cause. I died bravely, facing disease or sacrificing myself for others. I died for a cause greater than myself. The pretty girls who didn't notice me on the playground wept. I uttered goodbyes, last words that would comfort or haunt those I'd left behind. I closed my eyes and let the silence wash over me, my body still, wanting to feel the drift that would carry me to another world.

"When I was a child, I spake as a child, I understood as a child, I thought as a child. . . ." We are not children forever, at least not in the shackles of linear, A-theory time, and as we're forced to gaze upon the dark glass, our attitudes toward death change. We witness the car crash's shock and violence. We listen to the wheezing of pained breath, the sighs of pain. We feel for the confusion of the elderly. The child fantasizes about death. The adult understands death's reality is steaming toward him, a hurtling on the tracks of ever-faster time. The building vibrations sing in his bones. The headlamp's shine reaches closer. The whistle calls his name.

*

Time perception can be influenced by cultural and psychological factors, but there are new studies in brain research that indicate our most basic clocks are hidden beneath our bony skulls.

For years, it was a widely held belief that the brain's key structure in time perception was the cerebellum. But through their work with stroke patients and others with ADHD and Parkinson's Disease, researchers are turning their attention to the basal ganglia, a dopamine-rich core deep in the brain's base, and the parietal lobe located on the surface of the brain's right side.

Consider the ball bouncing between two plates, the metered passing of seconds. It's a balancing act, a trick that relies on perfect alignment. Consider the brain, the miracle of consciousness and thought, the greatest argument for God in this agnostic's life. Tick-tock says the realm of physical time, the rhythm man has imposed upon this world, and, if we're fortunate, our brains respond in time. *Tick-tock, tick-tock.*

*

The DSM-IV outlines specific conditions for a diagnosis of PTSD:

Criterion A—Stressor: the touchstone event itself, a situation of endured or witnessed brutality, and with it, a response of fear, helplessness, and/or shock.

Criterion B—Intrusive Recollection: a re-experiencing of the stressor event in the form of disturbing memories, nightmares, flashbacks, and/or distress following triggering events.

Criterion C—Avoidance/Numbing: a concerted effort to avoid reminders of the touchstone event, feelings of detachment, diminished interactions, and/or a general perception of a joyless future.

Criterion D—Hyperarousal: trouble sleeping, inability to concentrate, outbursts of anger, easily startled, paranoia.

Criterion E—Duration: symptoms in criteria B, C, and D last more than a month.

Criterion F—Functional significance: the disturbance causes significant impairment or stress in general life functions.

*

Billy Pilgrim cycled heedlessly through his own life.

Believers in reincarnation picture a soul cycling from one life to another.

Now take the concept of an eternal cycle and extend it across the cosmos, that highway of the Tralfamadorians who've witnessed not only their own deaths but the entire universe's destruction. The Stoics, jokers that they were, gave us *Ekpyrosis*, the belief our cosmos is destined to be destroyed by fire, an unimaginable conflagration every Great Year. After the fire, the universe rises, recreates itself, and is destroyed again.

The Great Year isn't a notion limited to the Stoics. NASA defines it as the time required for one cycle of the equinoxes around the ecliptic. Or about 25,800 years. Astrologers accept this time frame but view the procession through another lens—the equinoxes' slow march through the twelve houses of the zodiac. Other cultures give this period different names—the Yuga Cycle or the Perfect Year.

It the Stoics are right, the fire awaits. We will all be brothers and sisters with the people of Dresden.

*

But wait! Perhaps what was once science fiction can become reality. Perhaps our damaged souls can be soothed by a robot's programmed compassion and cool calculations.

Consider Ellie, a computerized system developed by researchers at USC and DARPA, the Defense Department's advanced research center. Ellie appears on the screen, an avatar of calm, a modestly dressed woman in a purple chair. Her hands folded on her lap. Her gaze patient and unwavering. The subject sits, and the session begins.

Ellie's voice is soothing, her silences sometimes awkward, the program implanted with long pauses to ensure she doesn't interrupt. Many veterans, wary at first, later say they found themselves at ease. Their confessions easier. A computer void of the prejudices and lenses we human types carry. Ellie's eyes look forward, part of a greater network of microphones and cameras, the subject's words only part of the collected data.

Ellie's real innovation waits in the realm beyond language. The program registers tonalities and modulations. It projects a blue web over the subject's face, a grid designed to deconstruct the elements of expression. Eyes. Mouth. The arch of an eyebrow and the tilt of the head. After all, not all smiles are the same.

Ellie analyzes the said and the unsaid and offers a screening of who might be suffering from depression or PTSD. The body betrays us—the soldiers not ready to name their demons. The body knows us before we know ourselves—the survivors of the children's crusades unaware of the fuses lit by the things they've seen and done. Ellie isn't a human replacement. She's a tool, a level of virtual intervention.

Why of course, say Vonnegut's old friends from Schenectady, New York. *Why of course*, say the Tralfamadorians and the adherents of eternalism. All of them understanding that the future is now.

*

"No evil is honorable; but death is honorable; therefore death is not evil."   —Citium Zeno

*

A 2011 study investigated the impact of emotion upon one's perception of time. Subjects were shown excerpts from movies and TV shows. The scenes fell into three categories—those which triggered fear (scary movies) or sadness (tearjerker dramas) or which were neutral (weather and stock market reports). Afterward, subjects were tasked with estimating the clips' durations. The sad and neutral clips had no significant impact on time perception, but the lengths of fear-inducing scenes were regularly overestimated. The researchers eyed our biological clocks, the elastic moments when one must choose fight or flight.

Poor Billy Pilgrim stepped from the slaughterhouse and into a horror movie. His minutes expanded, the hours stretching. His days spent walking among the dead reached into the future, a scene that would last forever.

*

"That which has been is what will be, That which is done is what will be done, And there is nothing new under the sun." —Ecclesiastes 1:9.

*

Dreaming, part II.

I'm lying in bed. My bed. My bedroom. I look to my left, the side with the room's only window. The east, the morning sun. There are pictures on the walls. The pictures are unframed, sketches on white paper. I'm not familiar with the pictures, yet I feel a connection to them. The pictures belong to me. I was involved with them, but I wasn't their creator. Was I?

I'm paralyzed. All I can do is turn my head. My gaze slowly pans left to right, east to west, and as I go, the pictures grow more crowded. The pages overlap, their edges rippling on a soft breeze. A few sketches evolve into jerky animations. I try to focus on these, but I can't stop my eyes' track across the room.

I realize the pictures, although unrecognizable, are moments from my life, and this pleases me. I reach the room's first corner. Then the wall opposite me, the pictures thicker here—three, four, five deep. I'm happy. I look down the center of my chest, and in that aligned moment, a pair of dark hands rise from the foot of my bed. With a wave, the pictures disappear. The hands turn to mist.

Something terrible has happened, but I must keep my eyes open. The pictures begin to return. They sprout, like seedlings in a time-lapse movie. There aren't as many, but I'm thankful for them and thankful also for the memory of the ones that existed before. I continue my scan, the room's western side, the pictures waiting, their details dimmed by the shadows.

A ribbon dangles into view. The ribbon rises, a lazy spiral, and at its end, a red balloon. I understand the balloon is my death. The balloon begins to sink, but I'm not afraid. The balloon reaches the floor, the hardwood coated in dust. The balloon deflates. Its red hue darkens, the color of blood.

*

Listen:

Kurt Vonnegut is dead. I will join him in my time. And not to spoil the suspense, so will you. So it goes. Until then, we will flow, alone and together, hello and farewell. When the current has had its way, we will be deposited on a distant shore. The flow will continue, absurd and random and unspeakably beautiful. Our only say against the fates waits in our choices. The decisions to be kind. To renounce the ugliness.

The best books are invitations. They are time machines. They challenge us to think, to reconsider. Behold Vonnegut's time machine, a narrative of a hundred different frames, a splintered perspective that lifts his whirligig contraption from the ground. He fuels his machine with man's weightiest elements—time, war, death—and then mixes an infusion of lightness, the spark of wit and irony. His machine rattles, taking flight with a shambling grace.

I am grateful to have returned to *Slaughterhouse-Five*. I've appreciated what I couldn't before, been touched in new ways. I'm a different person. I've loved and lost. I've married. I have a son. The young man who first read the book knocked at the door, asking his questions. Eternity. Meaning. The old man contemplates his bloody knuckles, the door as solid as it was all those years ago. He understands the only answers that mean anything wait in his heart and gut. All he can do is keep knocking.

Last week, my son finished *Animal Farm*, the final

chapters consumed in a post-bedtime grace period, his parents pushovers for such indulgences. The next day he announced he wanted to tackle *1984*. I hesitated, thinking of Julia's radical promiscuity, of the horrors waiting in room 101. I think of my walks to the bookstore of my youth, the image of my sneakers on the sidewalk. My son is on his own journey, his mind grappling with the tides roiling within and without. I make an after-work trip to purchase a copy of *1984* he can call his own.

Not long ago, my son was accustomed to having his questions answered. He asked, and we told him the distance to the sun and the age of the earth, how many feet were in a mile and the world's tallest waterfall. But children grow, and their questions change, and the answers don't come as easily. I can't explain why his grandfather died or why some find it easy to be cruel. No mathematical formula can rationalize prejudice or the ever-turning wheels of bloodshed.

I also buy a new copy of *Slaughterhouse-Five*, my original retethered in rubber bands and set back on the shelf, my repairs no match for the decades' toll. I'll shelf the new copy beside the old. Perhaps in the next few years my son will read the first few pages. Perhaps he'll accept Vonnegut's invitation and ride alongside Billy Pilgrim in his time machine. My son will finish the book, and the questions he'll have will be his alone.

I will tell him a secret—that I, too, struggle with the same questions.

I will tell him his is the gift of consciousness and free will, and that every day matters.

And the birds will join in their lovely and inexplicable chorus.

"Poo-tee-weet?"